Alex Carr was in a holiday mood...

...until he saw the ambulance parked in the Cunningham driveway. Two attendants were carrying a stretcher down the front steps.

"What happened?" Carr asked in a shocked voice.

"Heart failure," one of the attendants said as they passed.

The stretcher was lifted into the ambulance and the door was slammed shut. And that was the last Carr saw of Lloyd Cunningham, who had so recently dreamed of turning the entire country upside down—and who had told Carr exactly how he intended to do it.

Keeping you in suspense is our business

RAVEN HOUSE takes pride in having
its name added to the select
list of prestigious publishers
that have brought—in the
nearly one and one-half centuries
since the appearance of the
first detective story—the finest
examples of this exciting
literary form to millions of readers
around the world.

Edgar Allan Poe's
The Murders in the Rue Morgue
started it all in 1841.
We at RAVEN HOUSE are proud
to continue the tradition.

Raven House Mysteries

Let us keep you in suspense.

THE
AMAZON
FACTOR

William Wise

A RAVEN HOUSE MYSTERY FROM

W♦RLDWIDE

TORONTO · LONDON · NEW YORK

For Henry and Jane

Raven House edition published May 1982

Second printing

ISBN 0-373-63036-0

Printed in Canada

"While man can change his environment almost at will, he must be able to weigh knowledgeably the costs of change against the benefits.... The 1969–1970 HEW Task Force on Research Planning in Environmental Health Science noted that chemicals which are known or suspected of being harmful to human beings are being produced and marketed at an increasing rate. New products are being introduced into our society faster than their safety can be ascertained. Whereas these substances are aiding man in his development of a better life, they may also have insidious effects on his health."

Fogarty International Center
Conference Report
Mutagenic Effects of Environmental
Contaminants
DHEW Publication No. (NIH) 72-65

Prologue

"I BELIEVE you're worrying needlessly," the white-haired man complained. "He's only going to somebody's cookout. What makes you think it could lead to anything important?"

"I'm paid to worry," the man at the window said. "And I still don't trust our friend. My hunch is he's got something new up his sleeve. New and dangerous."

"Which means we finalize the back-up plan, and put it on hold?" The white-haired man looked thoughtful. "Well, it ought to work all right. Except there's really no guarantee he'll drink the water."

"The water won't be a problem. Whenever he feels tense, he takes one of his pills. So—we'll keep plenty of pressure on him—and he'll turn on the tap."

"And after that our good friend will be gone, and our worries will be over."

"*Might* be over," the man at the window said. "You never know what other difficulties could still crop up. And if they should, we'll just have to be flexible, and work out something else."

1

FOR THE FIRST HOUR OR SO it was a perfectly conventional summer party. Ed Slattery, their stocky, red-faced host, began to operate the outdoor grill; everyone seemed to be getting enough to drink, and as darkness fell, a few of the local mosquitoes finally bestirred themselves and made a preliminary sortie or two among the guests.

Carr had driven over with his sister and brother-in-law, but soon left them with some of their more convivial friends in order to circulate on his own. Catching sight of Eunice Slattery, he paused for an obligatory chat, and after complimenting her on the only thing he could think of on the spur of the moment—a string of notably ugly Japanese lanterns rocking gently above the lawn—drifted off by himself again.

It was while he was still standing alone in front of the outdoor bar with a fresh gin-and-tonic that he felt a hand clamp tightly around his elbow, and heard a voice with a slightly bogus English accent say rather breathlessly, "Alex—Alex Carr—I was hoping you might be here tonight. I've been wanting to have a talk with you all week."

Carr turned slowly in order not to spill his drink and stared up at the other man, who towered over him by at least half a foot. At first he was tempted to point out that anyone could have reached him during the week simply by picking up the telephone, but in-

w of gin and said, "Then
loyd. I'm certainly here, the
fect—no pun intended—and

yd Cunningham collected two
owed him over to the sprawling
end of the lawn where Lloyd's
wife, nding. It had been a month since
Carr had last her. Shadows concealed her face
now, but he remembered perfectly her long straight
black hair, lively blue eyes that were pale rather
than dark, and fine white skin that appeared to have
no blemish. They'd first met two years before, after
he'd moved to Walton. Thrown together at parties
like the Slatterys', they'd become casual friends—
until a month ago. Then, in a single evening, they
had surprised themselves, everything had changed,
and afterward she had insisted that they not meet
privately again—not until she was clear in her own
mind—at the same time, making no promises. And
without any other recourse, he had accepted her
terms.

It took Carr a moment to realize that his attention
had wandered, and that the other man had asked a
question. Luckily Ann had observed his lapse and
was filling in the silence.

"Busy? Of course he is. Writers are always busy,
whether or not they're actually writing. They have to
think and plan ahead. I'm sure they can't avoid it."

"Unfortunately you're right," Carr said. "Though
I must admit the season makes a difference. You
might say that summer idleness is my specialty. From
July Fourth to Labor Day, I always try to do as little
as possible."

"Then I think that this year," Cunningham said
gravely, "you really must learn to change your work
habits."

"Change them? Whatever for?"

"Because I have a story that's going to interest you, Alex. A remarkable story. Something I happened to stumble across a while ago at the hospital. A scandalous story that will turn this entire, misguided country of ours completely upside down."

Carr carefully studied the tall, gaunt man standing by the yew tree, but because of the shadows it was impossible to make anything out of his expression. Idly he wondered how many rounds the hospital administrator might have had before coming to the Slatterys', and whether excessive drinking had contributed to the Cunninghams' marital difficulties. And more immediately, he wondered what on earth he himself was supposed to say in response to such a bizarre pronouncement.

Humor seemed the most promising refuge. "Upside down, Lloyd? The entire country? Can any story possibly be *that* big?"

Cunningham wasn't to be deflected so easily, though. In an imperturbable voice he replied, "I can't swear to the exact shape and dimensions, but I do know it's going to be very big before it's done. Another Teapot Dome, I'd say, or perhaps another version of Watergate."

Ann remained silent, so Carr finally cleared his throat and said, "Then your idea is to clue me in on the story, and have me go ahead and write it?"

"Well, first there's some more digging to be done, Alex. The picture's not entirely clear yet, not by any means. Naturally I'll tell you what I've learned so far, and then I'm sure you'll want to start turning over a few rocks here and there, to see what—or who—comes crawling out."

"And after that?"

"Why, after that, when you've got to the bottom of things, you can put it together in any way you like, toddle off and pick up your Pulitzer Prize, and even thank me for my good offices if you should care to."

Carr took a long soothing swallow of gin, and then said, "It's a real pity, but I'm afraid you've got the wrong man for the job. I'm only a run-of-the-mill feature writer. I turn out articles for a couple of magazines, and occasionally do a book to help pay the rent. I'm not one of your brilliant young 'investigative reporters' who always makes such a splash. I don't turn over rocks, Lloyd. Scandal, political dirt or the latest sex-change operation just are not my beat. And worst of all, I've never cast a lustful eye in the direction of the Pulitzer. Not even once."

"But you *are* a journalist," Cunningham said. "And this is a great story."

"No doubt it is," Carr agreed hastily, "only not for me. Do you know what I'm scheduled to begin work on after Labor Day? An article about Hatshepsut, the Egyptian queen—dead for almost thirty-five hundred years. The only woman pharaoh who ever ruled successfully in ancient Egypt. Interesting, but hardly sensational. Quiet stuff, that's what I do."

Cunningham said nothing, so Carr went on, in what he hoped was a conciliatory voice. "All the same, I might be able to help you. Naturally I know a number of people in the field—writers and editors. Sometime soon you can fill me in on the background, if you like, and I'll try to think of the right person for you to see."

"I'm seeing the right person now," Cunningham insisted. "A stranger wouldn't suit me at all."

"That's understandable enough," Carr said.

"For one thing, I know I can depend on your judgment. I can count on your not going off half cocked, which could be extremely important. And Ann tells me you're an excellent writer. She's read your last book and any number of your articles. She agrees with me—you'd be much better than anyone else I could possibly find.''

Carr glanced from husband to wife before saying, ''I'm very flattered. But still unconvinced.''

There was another pause, and then Ann said, ''Lloyd, why don't you simply tell Alex what you told me the first night? Once you have, maybe he'll change his mind.''

''That's always possible,'' Carr said. ''I can't promise to take on the project, but I'd certainly be willing to listen.''

By way of reply Cunningham drew out and lighted a cigarette, and then expelled a turbulent cloud of smoke in the general direction of the nearest Japanese lantern. Finally he said, in what seemed genuine bewilderment, ''But I'd just assumed you'd snap it up, Alex. I can't imagine why you're acting this way. It's the chance of your professional lifetime, and here I am, practically on my knees begging you to take it.''

A second cloud of smoke followed the first. Then Cunningham sighed to himself and said, ''All right, maybe Ann's right. Maybe that's what I'll have to do.'' He looked down at them both and said, ''There are several things at the hospital, Alex, that I'll want to show you. Can you meet me there sometime on Monday? Say around ten o'clock?''

''Ten will be fine,'' Carr said.

''I'll be looking forward to it,'' Cunningham told him. ''Convincing a skeptic like you will be a pleasure. And after your apologies—humble and profuse—we'll finally be able to get down to business.''

A few minutes later Lloyd finished his drink, and when Ann said that she wasn't ready for another one yet, he excused himself and started back to the bar. Carr waited until Cunningham was out of earshot.

Then he said, "I don't suppose this is the best time for us to have a talk?"

"No, it isn't, Alex. Too easy for someone to over-hear us. And I'm not ready yet—I need a few more days. I told you not to pressure me."

"All right, then I suppose we'd better talk about Lloyd," Carr said easily. "He's really obsessed by this discovery of his, isn't he?"

"Totally. And has been for a couple of months."

"I suppose you know what it's all about?"

"No, if anyone does, it's certainly not me," she said with just a trace of bitterness in her voice. "I only know what he found out at the very beginning. One night he came rushing home from the hospital, so tense with excitement I thought he was going to burst out of his skin. After supper he pored over the encyclopedia. Then he phoned a math teacher he knows over at the college, but I didn't hear what was being said. Later, though, he seemed terribly pleased with what he'd learned."

"And then?"

"Then he clammed up completely."

"What an odd thing to do."

"Not for Lloyd," she said with a sudden laugh. "I'm afraid he likes mystification. He enjoys know-ing things that nobody else does—I suppose it gives him a feeling of importance."

"And he hasn't told you anything since?"

"Not a word. I asked once or twice, got the cold shoulder for my trouble, and simply stopped asking."

"So that actually you have no idea what he might have been doing the last few weeks? Or what else he might have learned?"

"I've no idea at all."

"Of course," Carr said, "I'd like to know what he did tell you that first night, but I imagine it would be better if I heard it directly from him."

"Much better," she agreed. "He'll certainly want to unveil the whole thing himself."

Carr fell silent for a few moments, while he thought about what she'd told him. Finally he said, "All the same, I am curious about your own impressions."

"I'm not sure I understand what you mean."

"Well, from what you do know, I wonder if you think that he might possibly have come across anything really...important?"

"Oddly enough," she said, "I think he probably has. Though it may not be quite as earthshaking as he seems to believe."

"Do you have any idea what kind of 'rocks' he'd like me to look under? Or what might be there?"

"Not the slightest. Except I imagine...." Her voice seemed to trail off into the darkness.

Carr heard a mosquito buzzing close by, and slapped carelessly at his neck. At last he said, "You were going to tell me something you'd been thinking."

She turned and walked a few steps away, until she was standing almost directly under one of the lanterns. "I suspect Lloyd's making a mistake. I imagine he thinks he's on the track of one thing, when in all probability he's been following something quite different. It's happened once or twice before. He'll go haring off after what he *wants* to find, and ignore everything that doesn't fit neatly into his theories."

"But you have no idea...."

"None. I've already told you that." She turned under the lantern, and for the briefest moment her face was bathed in an eerie and unflattering red glow. "Except that I have a feeling he might have stumbled across something evil."

"*Evil?*"

"That does sound melodramatic, doesn't it? Yet it's precisely what I feel. Evil, and possibly dangerous.

The kind of thing ordinary people, like the crowd of us here tonight, know very little about.''

Cunningham was returning from the bar now. Carr watched his head bobbing slowly above the other guests, and then he said to Ann, ''You'll call me soon?''

''As soon as I can. Lloyd and I have begun to talk. Finally.''

And then her husband loomed up beside them, before Carr could think of anything more to say.

2

THE CROWD OF GUESTS had already thinned considerably by the time Carr rejoined his sister, Joyce, and his brother-in-law, Arnold Daniels, on the back patio of the house, where they stood for several minutes completing their various goodbyes to the Slatterys. Then they walked slowly around to the driveway and got into the front seat of the Daniels's Cadillac.

"Christ, I ought to give up going to parties," Arnold said, making a sharp turn onto the dark country road. "Would you believe it—for thirty minutes I got buttonholed by that Argentine houseguest of the Wallaces. Wanted some free advice on his oil leases. Tax avoidance, naturally."

"I wish," Joyce said, "you'd drive more slowly, Arnold."

"Relax, sweetheart, I know these roads like the back of my hand. Thirty-two years without a ticket or a scratch. So I told the Argentine freeloader it was a tricky question, and he'd have to make a regular office appointment. Maybe English is only his second language, but he still got the message loud and clear."

"The legal life," Carr said, "does have its minor annoyances, doesn't it?"

"Just like the writing life. Say, where were *you* hanging out tonight? After we got there I hardly saw you. Making time with Eunice Slattery, I'll bet."

"Better than Eunice," Joyce said. "He was talking with poor Cunningham's wife. Darling, do you realize you're going over sixty? You'll make Alex so nervous he won't be able to sleep tonight."

"Why 'poor' Cunningham?" Carr asked, glancing for a moment at his sister's plump, good-natured face.

"Oh, I don't know," she said carelessly. "It's just the way I always think of him."

"Not entirely fair," Arnold said. "Not entirely accurate, either."

"Well, how would you describe Cunningham?" Carr asked him.

"Jesus, Alex, must we talk about that character tonight? Why the sudden interest anyway?"

"Because he thinks he's run across an important story and wants me to do it. I only wonder what I'd be letting myself in for."

"I can tell you in one word."

"Which is?"

"Trouble. *Tsouris*. Take my advice and head the other way."

Carr gazed out of the half-open window at a succession of tall black trees and dimly lighted houses that came whirling by. In another minute they'd be letting him off at the cottage where he had lived for the past two years, ever since Eve had died and he'd decided to give up the lease on their apartment and leave the city. The cottage would be empty, and suddenly he knew that he didn't want to say good-night, walk inside, and face the silence alone.

In a little while it would be all right again, but for the next half hour he needed company. So as they approached the last turn before the cottage he asked them to stop for coffee, and was relieved when the offer was accepted.

In a few minutes Carr had a tray and three cups of

coffee set out on the living-room table. Arnold took one without comment, and when Carr brought up Cunningham's name again, he merely scowled for a moment and then shrugged his heavy muscular shoulders. "All right, if you insist," he said. "I'll give you a rundown on him. As long as it's off the record."

"With you," Joyce said, "Alex *knows* it's always off the record."

"And maybe, sweetheart, I wasn't really thinking of Alex."

For a moment as he stared at his wife Arnold Daniels's dark face broke into a sly grin. Then he lighted one of his thin cigars, leaned his head back against the couch and said, "Okay—the facts on Cunningham. One, he's a first-class pest. Been making trouble ever since the day he came here. Two, he's slippery. Sometimes he'll give you a straight story, and sometimes he'll twist things a little, so you never can be entirely sure what's true and what isn't. Once he told me how he'd been on the Princeton swimming team, and set a slew of records in the backstroke. So the next time I happened to be over at the university I looked it up, and believe me, a Mark Spitz he wasn't. Till the middle of his senior year he was strictly junior varsity. Then half the squad came down with mononucleosis, so they let him swim in a couple of meets, and all but twice he finished dead last. As far as I could find out, the only record he ever set was for getting a leg cramp and almost drowning against Harvard."

Carr nodded and stirred his coffee. Finally he said, "What sort of trouble has Cunningham made since he came here?"

"Well, let me give you an example," Arnold said. "He'd only been in Walton about a year when he decided he didn't like the way our little town was being run. So he went around to the junior college, got some of the hippie types to register, and at the next election won three out of seven seats on the board of selectmen. You can imagine how popular that made him with the regular taxpayers.''

"And of course it didn't do any good," Joyce said, "because he never did win a majority. Now do you see what I mean by 'poor' Cunningham?''

"On the other hand," Arnold said, "he's not just a high-minded idealist, tilting harmlessly at a few local windmills. Far from it. Sometimes he can be damn smart. Too smart, in fact, for his own good. Like the time he got himself into hot water over those hospital explosions.''

"Hospital explosions?" Carr asked. "What are you talking about?''

Arnold tapped his cigar delicately against the rim of his coffee cup and a gray stump of ash dropped into the saucer. "I'm talking about a chemical compound called sodium azide. The stuff's completely harmless by itself, but when it's combined with lead or copper, it turns into either lead or copper azide, both of them highly dangerous explosives.''

"I think I remember what happened now," Joyce said. "It got into all the papers, didn't it?''

"All of them," Arnold agreed. "Which was exactly what Cunningham had in mind. You see, he'd been in touch with a chemical engineer out in the Midwest, and the fellow had told him a number of hospitals were beginning to install a new machine, known as an automatic blood-cell counter. Sodium azide is used in this machine. After the blood's been counted, there's a waste liquid from the process, which is placed in a holding tank and eventually flushed down the drain. If the pipes are old and rusty, there's a possibility the hospital's got some lead or copper azide in its plumbing system, instead of the harmless sodium.

"Well, this was meat and drink to Cunningham. He went out to some important health conference and really sounded the trumpets. He called in the press and read a paper on the subject. He claimed that all over the country tens of thousands of patients and hospital workers were in imminent danger of being blown sky-high by these explosives, and that a different kind of machine should be purchased immediately by the hospitals, to treat the wastes and eliminate the difficulty. His paper made lots of headlines. . . and damn near cost Cunningham his job.''

"Because he had the facts wrong?'' Carr asked.

Arnold took a swallow of coffee and shook his head. "No, it really wasn't the facts that got Cunningham into a jam. Of course he did exaggerate the danger, but reformers are always doing that to gain attention. And also he was a little premature in blowing the whistle. It took the experts quite a while to check out the situation, though when they did they said he certainly had spotted a potentially dangerous problem that needed some corrective measures.''

"Then it seems to me,'' Joyce said, "that Cunningham *was* right, and that he got a very raw deal.''

"Sure, you might say that,'' Arnold told her with a smile. "You might say he was a genuine hero who came to grief—except for one small detail.''

"Something to do with the law?'' Carr suggested.

"That's sharp, Alex. Very sharp.'' Slowly Arnold's smile faded, his shoulders seemed to sag, and his expression grew doleful. "One afternoon Cunningham came to my office in a terrific sweat. The headlines had been great, just what he'd wanted, but now he was in a serious jam. Nobody had realized that this chemical engineer in the Midwest had designed a machine to treat the hospital wastes, and it was this machine Cunningham had been hustling at the conference. Worse yet, our noble reformer had sent the engineer a check for five thousand dollars in exchange for a twenty-five percent interest in the device. An unscrupulous third party had got wind of the deal and was threatening to go to the papers unless he received adequate compensation."

"Why, that's nothing but common blackmail," Joyce said. "And Cunningham was just as wrong for what *he* did."

"Sweetheart," Arnold said, "you're right on both counts."

"And did Cunningham pay up?" Carr asked him.

"Let's just say that his attorney arranged a satisfactory settlement—the incriminating check disappeared—and the indiscretion of Walton's leading hospital administrator faded happily from view."

Arnold Daniels drank the last of his coffee and rose to go. "It's all in the past now, and—as I said before—off the record. But I thought it might give you an idea of what kind of a character you're thinking of dealing with."

Carr put on the porch lights and led Joyce and Arnold down to the road, and while his sister was getting into her side of the car, Arnold leaned out of the driver's window and said, "I didn't tell you that last bit about Cunningham just to pass the time, Alex. He really is a very slippery customer. Believe me, if you're supposed to get five thousand out of some story of his, he'll stand to make ten times that amount. He's public-spirited all right, but sometimes he confuses himself with the public."

"I've got the picture," Carr said. "And thanks for the information."

Joyce had climbed in on her side and now she slammed the door so that the overhead light went out and Arnold's face receded into the darkness. "Anyway," he added, "keep in mind what I've told you. And if you get a chance, let me know what you decide."

"I'll do that," Carr said. "And thanks again, Arnold."

The motor started, and a few seconds later two red taillights could be seen glimmering by the steep bend in the road. Then they vanished behind the curve, and Carr returned to the cottage, switched off the porch lights, and locked up for the night.

SLEEP DID NOT COME QUICKLY, though. At first he thought of Eve, remembering that once in the hospital she'd told him she expected him to marry again, she wanted him to someday. And then, after the memory faded, his mind turned to Ann Cunningham, and to the way that chance had drawn them together a month before....

It was June, the loveliest time of the year in Walton. For several days, afternoon and evening, they'd been working as volunteers, helping to prepare for the town's annual Library Fair. There were books to be picked up, booths to be prepared, donors to be thanked and, in between, a hasty meal to be shared. During that week an easy intimacy had stolen upon them, without either of them quite realizing it.

The night before the fair opened they decided to eat supper at a small café in town. It was late and they were both dead tired. Carr had a couple of drinks, downing them quickly. Over coffee, God knows why, they began to talk about famous women and what made them so memorable—Sarah Bernhardt, Cleopatra, Madame de Staël—was it exceptional intelligence, character, outstanding beauty—and Carr, looking across the table, suddenly said without thinking, "You're my idea of a beautiful woman, Ann."

For a moment her startled eyes looked into his. "I'm also a married woman," she replied.

"With a husband who doesn't seem to care where you are, or what you're doing."

"He's still my husband, though."

"Sometimes," Carr said, "a marriage doesn't work out."

There was a long silence, and then Ann said, "You're right, of course—why pretend? Lloyd and I have been having our troubles lately. But I don't believe in starting something new before you've finished with the old. Do you understand?"

He said he did, and they returned to the deserted library, worked for a couple of hours more, and then locked up for the night. He'd left his car in a garage that afternoon to have the carburetor fixed, and now she drove him back to the cottage in hers. Before getting out he looked at her and said, "I meant what I told you, Ann. You're a very beautiful woman. Since my wife died, there's nobody else I've said that to."

Something in her expression seemed to make his heart stop. Then she said, "Oh, God," and reaching out slowly, took his face in her hands and kissed him with a passionate hunger that told him more about the state of her marriage than any of her previous words.

Drawing away she said, "Alex, I meant what I said, too. My marriage with Lloyd hasn't been good for a long time. But I haven't decided to get out. Not finally. And unless—or until—I do I won't see you again. Not like this. I need a chance to think. To sort things out. So, if it really matters to you, you'll have to wait without pressuring me. Until I have something to tell you. Whatever it may be."

"All right then, I'll wait," he said. "For as long as I must."

And a month later, alone in Purley's Cottage, he continued to wait, though for what or for how much longer he still didn't know.

3

THE NEXT MORNING after breakfast Carr went out to the small untidy flower garden behind the cottage. At present it was decorated by a carelessly coiled garden hose, the eroded statue of a leprechaun, and a white plastic beach chair, into which he thrust himself with the Sunday papers.

The latest news items seemed as familiar as the summer sunlight: three hijackers had seized a plane over West Germany; a railway clerk in Belfast had been murdered by a pair of masked gunmen; nearer home, the F.B.I. was accused of unauthorized wiretapping on a vast scale, and from the summer White House came word that any further reduction in the Pentagon's budget would gravely endanger world peace.

Carr dropped the Sunday papers onto the grass. The air was warm and still, and the leaves of the towering sycamore at the far end of the garden hung motionless. His eye wandered over the scene without enthusiasm. Everywhere he looked there was work to be done. The lawn needed cutting again, and a half dozen overage rosebushes badly wanted pruning. Only Mr. Purley—his name for the hideous, grinning leprechaun—required no attention, which perhaps explained why he had never removed the eyesore from its place of prominence at the edge of the grass.

Later on, Carr decided, he would mow the lawn. Or

maybe he'd wait until the next day when there might be a breeze.

Committed to idleness himself, he began to speculate about the activities of others. How would they be occupying themselves on this sultry, lazy mid-summer morning?

Despite the heat, he was sure that his brother-in-law would be at the country club, engaged in a round of golf. Arnold was an interesting player. Cautious and competitive, he made few careless mistakes. Short off the tee, but straight down the middle. Never in the woods, seldom in the rough. Usually his opponent would outdrive him by twenty or thirty yards, yet afterward, when the bets were totted up, it almost always was Arnold Daniels on the collecting end.

How much could you tell about a man's character from the way he played golf? Probably not a great deal. Like the currently fashionable psycho-history, it would be a game with few rules, most of which you could make up yourself.

Two years earlier, at Arnold's suggestion, Carr had joined the country club. Membership came high, but Arnold had pointed out that he'd probably find it just about matched what he already was saving thanks to leaving the city and moving to the cottage in Walton. They rarely discussed financial matters, but that night they had, Arnold even conceding that he himself as a young man had found the cost of membership a considerable burden.

Such cares, of course, were well behind him now. Daniels and Daniels had been a modest enough business when he'd taken it over from his father, but since then he'd greatly expanded its activities. These days, not only was it Walton's principal legal firm, but Arnold had acquired a number of out-of-town clients, as well, whose interests demanded that he visit New York and Washington several times a month.

Sunday golf for Arnold, that was certain. But what about Joyce? Would she have gone to the club for a swim? Or would she have decided it was too hot, and so be back at the house, engrossed in the latest novel from her lending library?

Taking advantage of the summer light, Ann Cunningham surely would be at work, perhaps outside somewhere, perhaps in a studio at home. At one time somebody had said that she'd had several shows at a New York gallery, her style being either op art, minimal or neorealism. Today she'd be busy with tubes and brushes, and before long her pale skin would be flecked with red, or white or hideous green paint. . . .

Cunningham, a gaunt, brooding figure, would be alone in the garden. . . the vegetable garden. Down on his hands and knees, his long ungainly torso hunched over a pumpkin. . . .

Amazing what he was doing there. Taking papers out of the pumpkin and then muttering, "Secrets. . . secrets. . . secrets. . . . "

SOMEWHERE, FAR OFF in the distance, a faint insistent noise could be heard. Carr waited for it to stop, because it was an enormously vexing noise. Instead it kept repeating itself, until finally he awoke with a start to realize that inside the cottage the phone had been ringing for some time.

Even as he hauled himself out of the beach chair he felt sure the caller must be Cunningham, but when he picked up the receiver, it was his sister's voice on the line.

For several minutes she commented on the Slatterys' party, and then steered the conversation into a new channel. "Arnold was sorry," she said, "that he already had a golf date lined up for this morning. He'd have liked to play with you, I know.''

"I should have thought,'' Carr said, "that he'd seen enough of me for one weekend.''

"I think he wanted to talk about the Cunningham business. He's worried you might do something foolish.''

"Like taking it on?''

"He really thinks you shouldn't, Alex. He didn't actually come out and say so, but just the same, I know he finds the idea disturbing.''

"It's good of Arnold to be so concerned.''

"Well, I'm concerned, too,'' she told him. "Really, after what we heard last night, I do think you'd be much better off not getting mixed up with the man.''

"And so today you've decided to play big sister again?''

"Alex, dear, I wouldn't call it that. But when everything's said and done, I do feel—''

"Then *don't* feel. I'm several years the wrong side of thirty, and perfectly well able to handle my own affairs.''

"But are you, Alex? Well, of course you are, but still, I sometimes feel very anxious about you. I don't often let on, but I do know what the *real* trouble is.''

"And please—no matchmaking, either.''

"Have I said anything? Or mentioned anyone?''

"No, thank God. At least not this time.''

"Of course, I'm not blind, either. I saw perfectly well last night—but after all, when there's a husband in the picture—''

"I couldn't agree more,'' Carr said emphatically.

"Anyway, it's over two years since Eve died, so it's high time—at any rate I'd just like to see you a lot happier than you are.''

"Which means '*not being alone*'?''

"Of course.''

"And not taking on the Cunningham thing?"

"That, too, Alex. Now don't make fun of me. I only called because I have your best interests at heart."

"I know you do, Joyce. Which is very nice, and why I tolerate your meddling once in a while. But I really am a big fellow now, and I do manage all right for myself."

They talked no more of Cunningham, but agreed to have dinner later in the week whenever Arnold could fit it into his schedule. After that they hung up and Carr returned to the garden. He stared at the rosebushes and the leprechaun, and perhaps it was only a trick of the sunlight, but he had the impression that for a moment or two the wizened little man at the edge of the grass was regarding him with a particularly derisive smile.

4

EARLY MONDAY MORNING Carr left the cottage and walked outside to the low toolshed that also served him as a garage. He rolled down the windows of the red Volkswagen and drove into Walton, where he cashed a check at the bank and picked up his new eyeglasses from the optician's. Then he drove past the raw, treeless Junior College campus, and out to the Walton Hospital parking lot.

Just before ten he entered the four-story red brick building and gave his name to the middle-aged woman at the reception desk. He was asked to take a seat by the door, but when he did a number of recollections suddenly came flooding back, and for a moment or two his heart pounded heavily, and he felt sweat breaking out on his forehead.

There had been, he remembered, a similar reception room in the city hospital where he and Eve had been asked to wait until an attendant came to show them up to her room.... The day before, her doctor had told them that the cancer had spread further and the cobalt treatments would have to be resumed, and after a sleepless night she had packed a suitcase and they had come back to the hospital again. Wordlessly they had sat on just such a couch, and he had watched her fingers twist in her lap while he struggled without success to think of something to say that might comfort her, or ease his own sense of guilt and helplessness....

"Mr. Cunningham will be with you in a minute, Mr.

Carr," the receptionist said, and fixed him with a cordial smile he was at a loss to explain.

Gradually, though, as it always did, the past began to recede, and a few minutes later, by the time Lloyd Cunningham's tall figure had emerged from a nearby doorway, Carr felt almost himself again. Cunningham nodded, seized his hand and gave it a dramatic pump or two, and then with a faintly patronizing air, led him over to the reception desk.

"Alex, I want you to meet Carol Banner, our local traffic director," he said. "Carol, this is Alex Carr. As I'm sure you know, Mr. Carr is Walton's most eminent author, and it's our good fortune that he's agreed to write an article or two about us here at the hospital. I'm not at liberty to say just where the articles will appear, but I think we'll all be pleased with them once they're out. So whenever Mr. Carr decides to visit us again, I know you'll remember what I've said, and give him free access to inspect any hospital areas he might wish to see."

This introduction made, Cunningham led the way into the nearest corridor, and there said to Carr in a confidential voice, "I thought that was the simplest explanation to account for your being here. Now you can come over anytime you like without attracting attention. All right, let's start down this way, and I'll show you our setup."

For a man who soon planned to turn the entire country upside down, Cunningham proved suprisingly calm and unhurried as he conducted Carr to various points of interest around the hospital. Their leisurely tour of inspection included an introduction to several members of the staff, and an examination of the hospital's personnel department, its X-ray facilities, an empty operating theater, and the new intensive-care unit, of which, the administrator said, the entire hospital was extremely proud.

Finally Cunningham held open another door, and they entered the maternity wing. Almost at once Carr found himself being introduced to an invincibly cheerful young nurse named Edith Warner, and immediately afterward was obliged to admire seven or eight of her infant charges reclining in their nursery cribs behind the viewing window that separated them from the narrow visitors' gallery.

For several minutes, while Carr stared at the assembly of tiny wrinkled faces, Nurse Warner chatted enthusiastically with Cunningham about an impending shortage of blankets and a temporary breathing problem one of the infants had developed the night before. Having exhausted these professional topics, she told Carr that she looked forward to his next visit to the wing, and moved away on her round of duties. When she had gone Cunningham tapped Carr on the shoulder to gain his full attention. Then he said in a solemn voice, "It all began here."

"Did it really?" Carr said.

Cunningham nodded slowly. "We were standing right here in the visitors' gallery, when something she said started me thinking. I've been back to that morning any number of times. It's extraordinary how a chance remark could turn out to be so important."

"And what did she say that morning?" Carr asked him.

Apparently Cunningham did not choose to hear. "Absolutely extraordinary that a few idle words could ultimately make such a difference." Then he seemed to draw himself back to the present. He looked at Carr, and nodded toward the hall. "Let's go up to my office now," he said. "That's where the trail leads next."

Suppressing an urge to laugh at his solemn expression, Carr followed him down the corridor into a wide, slow-moving hospital elevator, and up to the top floor of the building. Once inside his office, Cunningham waved Carr to a chair, removed a metal drawer from the green filing cabinet that stood against the wall, and placed the drawer in front of him on the desk. Carr glanced down and saw that the drawer was labeled Walton Hospital, Obstetrical, Current, and that it contained twelve sets of alphabetized folders—a different set for each month of the past year.

"I'd like you to look through these records of ours," Cunningham said. "As you'll see, there's a separate folder for every birth we've had since this time last July, a full year ago. There are roughly four hundred folders—that being the number of births recorded in Walton during the time period in question."

"And I'll find something significant when I do?" Carr said.

"Precisely."

"No hints beforehand, though?"

"I don't believe you'll need any, Alex."

Carr shrugged, settled himself more comfortably on his chair, and bent over to examine the folders. He noted that they held a minimum of three documents: a white six-by-nine admission card, a record of treatment, and a Xerox copy of a birth certificate. Among other items, the documents listed the mother's name, her address, the name of the child's father and their social security numbers. Recorded, too, was the weight of the child, its sex, blood type, general health and any deficiencies or abnormalities observed, along with remarks concerning medication, diet, specific treatment of illness and, finally, the name and office address of the attending physician.

Carr read through the first folder carefully, without forming any idea what Cunningham might be driving at. The second and third folders proved equally unenlightening. As did the twentieth and the fiftieth, which he scanned more quickly.

"Breast feeding seems to be popular," he said, without looking up from the desk. "But I don't suppose that's it?"

"Hardly," Cunningham replied stiffly.

"And most of the mothers appear to be healthy. Very few complications. Am I getting warmer?"

"No. Not at all."

"Perhaps the names of the doctors...Barnett, Nussbaum, Wilson, Muchmore...Walton's corps of obstetricians, I suppose?"

"They are."

"A fact of considerable consequence?"

"A fact of no consequence whatever."

Leafing hastily through several more folders, Carr could discern no semblance of pattern or meaning. Names and statistics—they were there in abundance—but nothing more. Finally he said, "All right, Lloyd, I give up. I haven't the foggiest notion what you're getting at."

By now Cunningham had lighted a cigarette, and despite the efforts of the air conditioner, his office was growing smoky. "I'm disappointed, Alex," he said. "You're a damn clever chap, no doubt about it, so I was sure you'd get the point straight off. Still, I might not have been entirely fair to you. When I went searching I did have Edith Warner's remark to guide me. So I'll tell you what she said and then you can have another look."

Cunningham frowned and folded his hands together on the desk. "That morning in maternity," he said, "I was discussing some supply problems with Nurse Warner, and as we looked through the nursery window she said to me, 'I think we need some new nameplates, Mr. Cunningham. We're already pretty low on the pink ones. I don't know why, but maybe we've been getting more girls than usual lately.'"

"A curious idea," Carr said.

"Naturally, I thought so, too," Cunningham agreed. "At any rate, I was tremendously busy that day, so it wasn't until late in the afternoon that I remembered her remark. Then, even though I felt a perfect fool for doing so, I took out that same file drawer and ran through the folders. Four hundred of the damn things. And when I got done, I must confess, I'd never been more astonished in my life."

Carr bent down and began to examine the folders again. His eye ran over the infants' names—Catherine, Amy, John, Lewis, Martha, Lucy, Edward, another Amy, Michael, Alice. . . . Then he asked Cunningham for some paper and began to make a mark for each of the names, the girls in one column, the boys in another. When he'd finished marking and counting, Cunningham said, "How did you come out?"

"Girls, two hundred and forty-eight," Carr said. "Boys, one hundred and fifty-four. Which is nothing short of impossible."

Cunningham smiled for the first time. "Of course it is," he agreed, "unless we're not dealing with a question of pure chance, because some additional factor has become involved. As I'm sure you know, births tend to run about fifty-fifty, with a slight preponderance of males, so that what I'd discovered—as you've just pointed out—is a statistical impossibility."

"The odds would be staggering," Carr said. "I imagine it's like flipping a coin, and having that many heads come up. The chances of it happening would be at least fifty thousand to one."

Cunningham's smile grew broader. "Your mathematics are no better than mine were," he said. "That night I talked with someone I know at the Junior College, and was given the figure one followed by an endless series of zeroes—quite frankly, the number was beyond my comprehension.''

"And how do you account for it?" Carr asked.

At first Cunningham did not reply. Instead he stubbed out his cigarette, folded his hands again, and then looked thoughtfully at the opposite wall. Finally he said, "I'll explain that tonight, Alex, along with some of the other things I've learned. Oh, by the way, I took the liberty of telling Ann that you'd be over for dinner, and that the three of us would be celebrating your decision to accept the job."

"But I haven't agreed to anything of the sort," Carr told him.

"No, but you will," Cunningham said. "Because it's going to make a hell of a story, and you know it as well as I."

Carr shook his head quickly. "It *sounds* like it might make a hell of a story, Lloyd, I'll admit that much—but before I could agree to do anything, I'd certainly have to verify one or two points."

"Verify?" Cunningham said blankly. He thought for a moment, and then he began to scowl. "Verify what, if I may ask?"

"The figures we've been talking about. How do I know for sure they're authentic?"

"Are you suggesting that I've distorted them in some way?"

"Possibly. It wouldn't have been too hard. All you'd have had to do was extract a number of the folders this morning before I came—those with some of the boys' records in them—and then feed me a story about getting an unbelievably large surplus of baby girls."

"My God," Cunningham said, "you are a cynical bastard, aren't you? It must be your profession. I suppose, sooner or later, every bloody journalist comes to suspect whatever he hears."

"Well, we do learn to have our little doubts," Carr said. "But I wouldn't take it personally. It's just a routine precaution. Today I'll try getting in touch with one or two of your obstetricians, and I'm sure their office records will bear you out. Then I'll look into a couple of other corners if I can, and after that—since no doubt what you've told me is completely true—I'll be reasonably sure of my ground."

"And then what?" Cunningham asked.

"Why, if you'd still care to have me over, I'll come for dinner tonight, and we'll be able to discuss the matter rationally and see what can best be done."

"Jesus, I don't know why you're giving me such a damn hard time," Cunningham sighed. He took out another cigarette, thought better of it, and returned it to the pack. By then his frown was gone, and seemingly his resentment, as well. "All right, we'll see you tonight," he said. "At seven-thirty. I'll be looking forward to it."

Cunningham offered to see him down to the front desk, but Carr assured him that he would have no difficulty finding his way out, and left the hospital administrator standing by the elevator. Instead of going directly to the ground floor, though, he got off on the second, and walked slowly into the maternity wing.

By the time Nurse Warner came by, Carr already had a pad and pencil in his hand and was busy jotting down notes, "I wonder," he said, "if you could spare me a moment or two? You see, for these articles, I'd like to be able to start with a human-interest touch, maybe something about the way parents select their babies' names, and I thought it would be a tremendous help if you could supply me with the names of the babies you have here now."

"Easiest thing in the world," Nurse Warner said. "No problem at all."

He followed her to the floor desk, where she found

a list of her chrges, and then, in a sing-song voice, she began to read off their names. "Clara, Odette, Mary-Ellen, John, Sarah, Claudia, Peter and Kim."

Carr scribbled furiously. "Is Kim a boy or a girl?"

"A girl."

"Rather a tidy majority of girls today, isn't it?"

Nurse Warner nodded placidly. Then a thought struck her—perhaps the first one that day—and her vacant expression turned to one of surprise. "Do you know, that's real funny," she said to Carr. "A couple of months ago, I told Lloyd—Mr. Cunningham—the same thing. 'We're running out of pink nameplates, so we must be getting more girls than usual.' That's what I said to him."

"Well, you know about the law of averages," Carr said. "If you actually have been getting more girls, sooner or later things will turn around, and then you'll start getting more boys for a while."

"The law of what?" Nurse Warner said blankly. For a moment she struggled with the problem, but then apparently grew weary of the effort. "Of course, I guess you're right," she said with a cheerful smile. "I hadn't thought of that. Anyway, baby girls are just as nice as baby boys, so what difference does it make?"

Carr nodded, thanked her for her help, and then moved off to the elevator. At least he knew one thing already—either young Edith Warner was the most accomplished liar he'd ever met or else, for one of the few times in his life, Lloyd Cunningham was telling the complete and unvarnished truth.

5

CARR'S FIRST STOP after leaving Walton Hospital was at Dr. Alvin Barnett's spacious, well-furnished offices on Palmer Street. Here he presented himself as a medical journalist, engaged in research on certain clinical aspects of early child care. Aided by an official-looking membership card in the Authors' Guild, which he deftly extracted from his billfold, and by the earnest manner and reassuring smile that were no small part of his stock-in-trade, Carr soon had gained access to the doctor's current records. He found that during the past year Dr. Barnett had brought forty-three of his patients successfully to term. In twenty-five cases the mother had delivered a baby girl, and in eighteen, a baby boy.

The office records of Drs. Nussbaum, Wilson and Muchmore revealed a similar picture. And when Carr had added up the figures, he found that Walton's four obstetricians had delivered 248 girls, and 154 boys—exactly the figures he'd gathered earlier that morning from Cunningham's hospital files.

Leaving Dr. Muchmore's office, Carr stopped at a lunch counter near the junior college for a hamburger and a Coke, and then drove along the recently completed highway extension to Bridgeville, the county seat. At the Hall of Records he produced his Guild card again and was shown to a remarkably uncomfortable wooden chair in a gloomy, secluded cubbyhole on the second floor, where, for the rest of the

afternoon he painstakingly examined local population statistics and the births recorded that year in
Hamilton County.

He discovered a number of interesting facts at the
Hall of Records. The residents of Walton itself, and
the areas clustered around it, comprised about a
third of the entire county's population. During the
past year, births in the town and its immediate surroundings had been radically out of balance, as Cunningham had claimed. And the phenomenon had
been confined exclusively to the Walton area. The
rest of Hamilton County had not suffered any imbalance whatever. Clearly the trouble was in Walton
itself and its immediate neighborhood, while a few
miles away the effects of the strange "plague" had
not been felt at all.

Because of this, only one conclusion was possible:
call it a phenomenon, a plague, or what you would—
something bizarre had made its appearance in
Walton itself, and apparently still was present there
in full force.

At four-thirty a young man with a thin red beard
informed Carr that the Hall of Records was about to
close, and so he shut up his attaché case, walked
back to the Volkswagen and drove out of Bridgeville.
He returned to Walton at a leisurely pace, taking
Route 23, a winding back-country road that led to
the bridge over the Penn-Central railroad tracks.
There it turned, and after a mile or two, went past
some of the large estates near the country club, until
eventually it twisted down the steep hill and around
the sharp bend that led to Purley's Cottage.

Once the Volkswagen had been put away in the
shed, Carr checked his answering service and
learned that his agent, Mark Watson, had called him
from New York to confirm their appointment for Friday lunch. His sister had also left a message, saying

that Arnold would be able to have dinner on Thursday.

Carr took a shower and, after toweling off, stretched out on the living-room couch to collect his thoughts. Having been forced to accept the truth of Cunningham's story, he now found himself faced with a number of new and tantalizing questions. One thing, of course, came before everything else—what kind of phenomenon had the hospital administrator stumbled across? Was it a disease, an infection, or the result of some environmental accident? Had the problem existed for more than a year, and had something similar occurred in other places around the country? How much had Cunningham already learned? And how much remained to be tracked down and revealed? Enough for a blockbuster book that would bring a sharp gleam of approval to Mark Watson's usually sober eyes?

Carr got up and began to dress for dinner. As he slipped his arms into a gaudy summer sports jacket, he asked himself two final questions. Why had Lloyd Cunningham failed to announce his discovery at once? And what did he now hope to gain from disclosing the fact that in the lovely suburban community of Walton, New Jersey, infant girls were appearing in unusual numbers, while infant boys—though not yet an endangered species—were nevertheless becoming curiously scarce?

6

THE CUNNINGHAMS lived on Willow Brook Lane, about a quarter of a mile from the blacktop road that ran from Purley's Cottage to the railroad station. It was not a part of Walton that Carr had visited before, but he found the house easily enough by following Cunningham's detailed instructions.

Even as he parked the Volkswagen, though, he saw how completely he had misjudged Ann Cunningham's surroundings. The house was a conventional split-level, one of a dozen or so standing in a double file on either side of a cheerless, unfinished-looking suburban street. Despite its low hedge and other plantings, the house was utterly devoid of privacy. As far as he could see there was no separate studio for a painter to retreat to, and for that matter, nothing visible among the other houses in the development that any painter in his right mind would want to set down on canvas.

Cunningham came out to meet him at the curb and then led him around to the back of the house, where there was a well-tended lawn and a narrow, unroofed patio. A garden sprinkler was energetically flinging out spray across one corner of the lawn, while on a feeder close to the house two or three sparrow-size birds were noisily putting away a final meal before the dusk deepened further and turned into darkness.

Ann was standing on the patio. She was wearing a

pair of black slacks and a long-sleeved scarlet shirt. When she gave him her hand he glimpsed a thin gold chain around her throat, and he caught a trace of her perfume before she turned away.

A round metal table, three chairs and a wine cooler had been assembled on the patio. Glasses and some hors d'oeuvres stood on the table. Cunningham announced that this was a special occasion—Carr's first visit to their sylvan retreat—excused himself, and went into the house, evidently to uncork a bottle of wine. Ann watched him go, and then said, "Lloyd tells me you've spent the day checking his story?"

Carr nodded.

"He seems quite sure that you'll take on the job."

After staring at her for a moment, Carr said, "I haven't found any good reason not to."

"Then I'm sure he'll be pleased."

"And you?"

"I'll be pleased, too, of course," she said, but before she could add anything more, Cunningham returned to the patio carrying a towel wrapped around a bottle of champagne. He filled their glasses and proposed a toast. "To the future," he said, "and to what I trust will be many more equally pleasant visits."

They tried the champagne, and then while Ann began to dispense the hors d'oeuvres, Lloyd Cunningham cleared his throat nervously and said, "Well, old man, how did things go after you left my office? I assume you checked with Nussbaum, Muchmore and company. Did they give me a clean bill of health?"

"One hundred percent."

"And after that?"

"I drove over to Bridgeville, and spent the afternoon in the Hall of Records."

"So you thought of that, too?" Cunningham said. "You really are a quick study, Alex."

"Well, it *is* my line of work, isn't it? Knowing how to check into things, and then setting them down on paper. I imagine that's what you'll be expecting me to do."

"Ah—then you *will* come in on it?"

There seemed no point in delaying further, so Carr said, "As long as we can work out a reasonable agreement—some sort of contract to cover the work involved, and to avoid any misunderstanding later on about dividing the royalties—why yes, I'll be glad to take on the job."

Cunningham got to his feet and circled the table, then poured more champagne. Then came a second toast, ending with an extravagant tribute to Carr's professional skills and general intelligence.

Clearly Cunningham was relieved. He excused himself, went into the house, and returned with a glass of water. Then he drew a tiny bottle from his jacket pocket, uncapped it and swallowed one of the pills it contained.

His gaunt face looked unnaturally pale. Catching Carr's eye, he said, "My digoxin, old man. Same thing as digitalis. Recommended for chronic heart insufficiency—or what they used to call in a less pretentious age, a tired ticker. Whenever I've been under a strain for too long, I have to take the bloody stuff. And God knows, Alex, the way you've been dragging your feet since we first talked at the Slatterys', I have been under a bit of pressure, haven't I?"

Before Carr could think of a suitable reply, Cunningham threw back his head and roared with laughter. "But that's all over now," he said. "Tonight we can get down to cases. I have a lot to tell you both, so why don't we go inside and I'll start to fill in the picture."

They left the patio and walked through the kitchen to the dining room, where the table had been set for three. Soon there was a platter of cold poached salmon on the table, an avocado-and-tomato salad, hot garlic bread and a bottle of chilled white Burgundy. The room was cool, a result of an air conditioner humming quietly in a corner window. An oil painting and several watercolors decorated the walls. Landscapes, mildly abstract, presumably the work of his hostess.

By the time they had begun to eat, Cunningham seemed more like his usual self again. His skin had regained some of its normal color, and his accent had become, if anything, even more British.

"As you know," he said, "at the very beginning I was totally stunned by what I'd discovered in the files. A great dearth of boys during an extended period of time—for all practical purposes, a mathematical impossibility—and yet demonstrably true. Quite certainly something extraordinary had been taking place in our community, and I felt it was my responsibility to find the explanation."

"Unless you decided to go to the health authorities instead," Ann said with an ironic smile, "and let them investigate the problem through normal channels."

"Dealing with bureaucrats," Cunningham said with a frown, "is seldom the best way to get things accomplished."

"Or you might have gone straight to the newspapers. After all, whatever the explanation, you certainly had got hold of a headline story, and no doubt they'd have been interested."

Cunningham frowned with even more irritation. "Naturally I considered doing that," he said, "but I soon had second thoughts. As you may possibly remember, Ann, I *have* had dealings with the press, and I've learned to my sorrow that your average reporter is an extremely skeptical animal. I knew I'd be subjected to considerable scoffing at first, if not outright ridicule—only look at Alex's initial reaction the other night at the Slatterys'. As a result, I felt sure that unless I had a good deal of the story actually in hand, I'd be put through a needlessly trying time before anything could come of it.

"Besides," he continued, "I had another reason for holding back. Knowing the world as I do, I suspected that some extremely powerful interests might very well be behind what was taking place, and if I was right but failed to learn *precisely* who the responsible parties were, any newspaper investigation would inevitably turn into a whitewash. So I decided to stay on my own for a while, and see just how much I could unearth before going public."

"And where did you begin?" Carr asked.

"With a single, basic assumption," Cunningham replied. "Considering the incredibly polluted world we live in today, it seemed all too certain that Walton had experienced some sort of 'environmental insult,' and that without realizing it—through our food, our water, or the air we breathe—we had taken into our bodies a massive dose of some injurious chemical pollutant."

Cunningham rose, picked up the bottle of wine and started to refill their glasses. "Hundreds of such chemicals," he said, "are all around us, chemicals that literally did not exist ten or even five years ago. They're being manufactured and put to commercial use without sufficient testing, and as a consequence, without anyone knowing what undesirable side effects they may turn out to have.

"D.D.T., of course, we all remember. P.C.B.'s—polychlorinated biphenyls is the technical term for them, I believe—are another horror story. As you know, in Japan, they were found to cause numerous birth defects and other personal injuries. And now, it seems, a new bit of chemical wizardry has been visited upon us here in Walton, with a singular and bizarre effect. Evidently *our* contaminant contains an 'Amazon Factor,' an element that does not affect a woman's body, but which, upon entering the body of a mature male, settles in the testicles and immobilizes or destroys the Y chromosome in the man's sperm. As you know, I'm sure, if you eliminate the Y chromosome, a couple can produce nothing but female offspring, and that clearly is what has been happening here, to a number of our unfortunate townspeople."

"But why," Ann said, "has this Amazon Factor of yours affected some men and not others?"

Lloyd Cunningham held his glass aloft and gazed affectionately at the contents. "You've hit on the key question—and one that puzzled me for a considerable time. I thought that the answer might be found in the files themselves, and so, in my spare hours, I kept running through them, searching for the vital clue.

"At first I separated the fathers of girls and the fathers of boys into two groups, and looked for a critical difference between them. I thought that quite possibly the age of the fathers or the state of their health might be of significance. But I was mistaken—the age and the general health of both groups were the same. Then I looked at the occupation or the educational level of the fathers, and again I drew a blank.

"So I tried a new tack. Might not some of the fathers have commuted to work and been affected somewhere else? In Philadelphia, say, or in the New York-Newark area? Well, at considerable inconvenience I obtained the names of the fathers who regu-

larly worked out of town, and discovered that they
had sired girls and boys in equal numbers.

"I really was at my wit's end," Cunningham said
with a sigh. "I felt utterly baffled—that was the only
term to describe it. And then, late one afternoon at
the office, I had another idea. Could there be something significant in the location of the affected
families—in the places where they lived? I had a map
of the Walton area, and now I began to stick pins in
it—a white pin for each infant girl, and a black one
for each infant boy. And when I'd finished, I'd found
the solution. In one area of Walton there were just
three black pins—and ninety-eight white ones. Only
a quarter of the town had been affected—or should I
say devastated—while the other three-quarters, with
three hundred births, was producing children at the
usual fifty-fifty rate."

"I wonder," Ann said, "how come there were
even three boys? In what way were their fathers different from the others in the same area?"

Cunningham smiled, and drained off the last of his
wine. "I wondered myself," he said. "So I thought
the matter over briefly, and then went to Eunice
Slattery for assistance."

"Good God," Carr said, "why ever to her?"

"Because, old man, she's Walton's most active and
successful real-estate agent, and I had a hunch she
might know the families in question. As it turned
out, I'd made a lucky guess. Hardworking Eunice
was well acquainted with all three. She'd shown
them a number of houses, and what was more important, she knew to the day when they'd first come to
Walton."

"And that was quite recently, wasn't it?" Ann
said.

"In every case," Cunningham replied, "within the
last six months. So that it's absolutely certain the

three boys were conceived in some other place, well before their fathers had settled in the afflicted part of our community."

By now they had finished eating and at Cunningham's suggestion they went outside to have their coffee on the patio. A light breeze had sprung up, and the air was considerably cooler than it had been before. At the far end of the lawn the garden sprinkler made a gentle whooshing sound as it revolved slowly in the dark, while overhead the first stars gleamed softly in the night sky.

Aware of the pleasant effects of the wine, Carr slowly stirred his coffee and thought over what the other man had told him. Finally he said, "All right, Lloyd, I think I've got the general picture. Now I'd like to know what else you've been able to learn. Have you found out, for instance, when the trouble started? Or what the source of the contamination might be?"

"The trouble began a little over a year ago," Cunningham replied. "Before that, births were following a completely normal pattern here, and naturally enough the same held true for the rest of the surrounding area. I might add that at no time have any other parts of Hamilton County been the least affected."

"So that unquestionably the problem exists in a section of Walton, and nowhere else?"

"No doubt of it," Cunningham said. "But merely for the time being, of course. I can't prove it quite yet, but I'm reasonably certain that we're only seeing the tip of the iceberg now. Before very long, if my suspicions are correct, what's happened here will be repeated, though on a less dramatic scale, throughout the rest of the country. The United States will wake up one morning to find that it's on the way to becoming a nation with a serious imbalance between the sexes. And when that happens the American people will be up in arms, and some very important business and political leaders will be called to account.''

Before either of his listeners could comment, Cunningham excused himself, went over to the side of the house, and turned off the water. Then he ambled down to the end of the lawn, picked up the sprinkler, and carried it to a new location. Returning to the house he switched on the water again, and finally came back to the patio and sank into his chair.

After a moment's silence he looked at Carr and said, ''You asked me whether I'd learned what the source of the contamination might be. Well, let me tell you what I've discovered so far. Since I knew when the trouble had begun in Walton, I did the obvious thing—I searched through the local papers for some sort of minor industrial accident. I felt reasonably sure that such a mishap had occurred a little less than two years ago, probably at one of the four small drug or chemical plants that are located in our general vicinity, and that the contaminant had spilled out of a storage tank or the like, escaped into the ground, and entered a part of our water supply. These circumstances—rather than an air pollution episode, for example—would best explain why the Amazon Factor has affected us here, and yet has not affected men in a wider area. When I found that such an accident had indeed occurred at the A. and S. Chemical Company almost two years ago—and about a year before our birth patterns began to change—I was satisfied that I had no need to look further for the source of the trouble.''

''What kind of chemical was it?'' Carr said.

''According to the company, an ordinary nitrogen compound, widely used in the production of certain fungicides.''

"Which you do not happen to think is true?"

"On the contrary—which I'm sure is completely true."

"Is A. and S. a publicly held corporation?"

"No, it's a small, privately owned outfit—and a very interesting one, I might add."

"What makes it so interesting?"

Cunningham took out a cigarette, lighted it and drew in a lungful of smoke. Then he said in an amiable voice, "But that, old boy, is one vital matter I'm not yet ready to discuss."

Carr was unprepared for Ann's reaction. She clapped her hands together in exasperation and cried, "Christ, Lloyd, when are you going to stop this damn cat-and-mouse nonsense and begin to act like a reasonable human being?"

There was just enough light on the patio to make out Cunningham's expression. "I'm afraid, my dear," he said with a self-satisfied smile, "that what's sauce for the goose is also sauce for the gander. There was nothing wrong with Alex's doubting my integrity, was there? You didn't object to *that*—yet now you object when I show signs of doubting his."

"I think you're being childish and absurd."

"Well, perhaps I am. But as far as I'm concerned, trust is a two-way street. So until we've drawn up and signed our little agreement, I'll just keep the rest of my findings to myself, and then Alex won't be tempted to take our story and go off on his own."

Cunningham swung around and said to Carr, "I hope you won't mind waiting, but once the document's signed and sealed, my information will be entirely at your disposal. Names, dates, the whole lot. All put down on a number of tape cassettes I've been recording faithfully for the past several weeks.

As soon as the ink is dry on the pact, out they come from my safe-deposit box, and over they go to you."

Perhaps it was the excellent wine he'd been drinking—or the generous amount of it—but in spite of himself, Carr felt vastly tolerant and amused. He laughed and said, "All right, Lloyd, I'll go along with your goose-and-gander bit. You keep the dossier till I can talk with my agent and get him to draw up an agreement between us. Another few days and then you won't have anything to worry about."

"Another few days?" Ann said sharply. "And in the meantime, what about the people who live around here? Are more families going to be poisoned while you two business types haggle over a deal?"

"There's no point in getting upset," Cunningham told her. "Believe me, the damage has long since been done. A few days one way or another won't make any appreciable difference to the people in Walton, and it certainly won't save the rest of the country from what lies ahead."

Cunningham offered him a brandy but Carr declined, saying that he'd better think about starting for home. Ann scarcely seemed to notice, and a few minutes later when he stood up to leave, she said goodbye without any particular warmth and did not accompany him beyond the front door.

After they'd reached the curb, Carr climbed into the Volkswagen and then looked up at the other man. "You know, Lloyd," he said, "at the very least it's going to stir up quite a fuss. If we can make it stick, everybody from Nader's Raiders to the Sierra Club will haul out their placards and take to the streets. Not to mention the hundreds of personal-injury suits that will be filed against the manufacturers."

"Of course, old boy," Cunningham said with a complacent smile. "As I told you over at the Slatterys', it's a scandalous story that's going to turn the entire country upside down.''

"I think it might do a good deal more than that.''

"What do you mean, Alex?''

"Well, if you're right about the extent of the problem—if Walton really is only the tip of the iceberg—think of what that would eventually mean. In another few years we'd begin to have a shortage of police and firemen in our towns and cities, not enough young men to serve in the armed forces, and a shrinking pool of men for American women to marry. Let the problem really be nationwide—and let the news of it get out—and the country would be faced not simply with another Teapot Dome or Watergate, but with an international political crisis, as well—one that might ultimately threaten to undermine the power of the United States itself, with the most appalling consequences for the entire free world.''

An unexpectedly high-pitched laugh escaped from Cunningham. "You know, Alex, you're absolutely right. I've been concentrating so much on the short-term considerations—find the culprits, pin the blame on the hidden malefactors—that I believe I've overlooked some of the more interesting long-term implications. It's a good example, isn't it, of how one can lose sight of the forest for the trees? Really, what you're suggesting could be much bigger than another Watergate. We'll have to discuss the whole thing further when we have more time. But I do like the sound of it already. Trust a professional writer to take the long view, and to see the full range of possibilities.''

Cunningham tittered again, and Carr was reminded, incongruously enough, of a small boy expressing his inward glee over some recently perpetrated mischief. He saw Cunningham raise his

arm in a comradely salute, and then he himself sent
the Volkswagen off through the darkness. And as he
drove away he felt a twinge of uneasiness at having
struck a bargain with such a curious person—a man
who could giggle with delight at the idea of an impending national crisis or an international political
disaster.

7

THE NEXT DAY Carr telephoned Mark Watson in New York and made arrangements to meet for an early lunch on Friday. He was tempted to tell his agent about Cunningham and the situation in Walton, but decided it would be wiser to wait till the end of the week when he could tell him in person over a couple of stiff drinks.

As the hours passed he felt increasingly restless. Yet until he'd listened to Cunningham's tapes there was little he could do to settle his own doubts or map out an intelligent course of action. Exercise seemed the most sensible escape. He went to the club and spent the rest of the afternoon hiking up and down the sloping hills, his mind preoccupied with everything that had occurred since he'd gone to the Slatterys' cookout the previous Saturday. Unable to concentrate, he sprayed shots all over the landscape and returned to the pro shop with his worst score of the summer.

After a shower and change he drove into town to shop for groceries. A young mother stood directly ahead of him in the checkout line. She was wearing a T-shirt and Levis. In a sling on her back she carried a small child, whom she'd wrapped up snugly like an Indian papoose. The edge of the child's summer blanket was just visible over the top of the sling, and Carr was not surprised to see that it was a pale shade of pink.

Having picked up his supplies, Carr drove back to the cottage and ate a solitary supper. Later he telephoned his sister, Joyce, and fixed a time and place for Thursday dinner. Then he read some of Breasted's *History of Egypt* until he was tired enough to sleep.

DURING THE NIGHT it began to rain, and Wednesday dawned damp and misty. By early afternoon, though, the air had cleared and the sun again was burning in the summer sky. After looking at the neglected garden, Carr decided to put a few things in order. He went to the shed, found a pair of rusty shears, and walked down to the end of the grass to trim the rosebushes. He'd just finished dropping a dozen thorny stalks into a garbage bag, when he heard the bell ring. Padding through the living room he tugged at the front door, but it was swollen with dampness. Finally, after a sudden wrench, he flung it open.

Ann Cunningham stood on the porch, looking pale and drawn. "I can only stay for a minute or two," she said. "May I come in?"

He opened the door wide and followed her into the living room, where he threw aside a few books and offered her a chair. His throat felt painfully dry as he said, "A month can seem like a long time, Ann. I'm glad you've come."

"Alex, please—I know you've been patient," she said quickly. "But I'm not really here to talk about us."

"Nothing's been settled then?"

"Only the preliminaries. I've agreed to give Lloyd a divorce, but I haven't even been to a lawyer yet. And there's still the problem of selling our house, and where he'll be living in the meantime. *Now* he's talking about moving out and setting up housekeeping with his girl friend, and in a town like Walton...."

"I'm sorry it's been so rough," Carr said.

"Well, anyway, the worst part is already over. I was going to tell you in another few days, after I'd pulled myself together a little."

She was sitting close enough to be able to reach out and take his hand. "And knowing that you cared what was happening," she told him with a smile, "made it a whole lot easier."

He nodded, and then said, "I guess old habits die slowly, and I've always hated unsolved questions. So—since you didn't come here to talk about *us*— why did you come?"

"Because of Lloyd," she said. "He's double-crossing you, Alex. I don't know how or why, but that's what he's doing."

"Double-crossing me?"

"He's already made a deal with somebody else."

"Another writer?"

She shook her head firmly. "No—it can't be that."

"Look, take your time, start at the beginning, and then maybe we can get some of this unsnarled."

To his surprise, her cheeks suddenly turned a furious shade of red. Then she said, "Oh, damn it, Alex, this is going to make me sound even worse than I really am."

"It can't be that bad. And I'm not a kid, you know. I've been married myself, so a lot of it won't be news to me."

She nodded gratefully. "I learned about it last night," she said. "It was after supper, and I didn't know if Lloyd was in his study, or whether he'd gone out. I'd been stretching canvas, and when I'm working I lose track of him completely. Suddenly the phone started ringing, and I picked it up. Before I could say anything, he picked up the extension. I was sure he hadn't heard me, so instead of getting off, I stood there and listened."

"What happened then?"

"They began to talk. Lloyd and a man named Ritter."

"You're sure of the name?"

"Yes, that's how he started. 'This is Ritter.' At first Lloyd sounded upset. 'I've asked you not to call me here,' he said. 'It's too risky.'"

"And then?"

"The other man said, 'Well, I had to. It's been more than a week since I've heard anything. Have you got that writer signed up yet?'"

"Do you remember any more?" Carr said.

"Not much. Lloyd told him he had the writer under his thumb, and in another few days everything was going to be fine. And then they rang off."

"Do you know anything about this man Ritter?"

"Nothing."

"Lloyd's never mentioned him?"

"No."

Carr thought for a moment, and then said, "Ever heard Ritter's voice before?"

"Not that I know of. It was a funny voice, though."

"Funny how?"

"Well, I don't think he's an American. Not born here, I mean."

"Would you say European?"

"I think so."

"How about the call? Was it long distance or local?"

"It sounded local. But I can't be absolutely sure."

Carr sighed and shook his head. "Well, there isn't much to go on, but maybe I can find out something about him. I'll ask my brother-in-law, Arnold Daniels. He knows everybody in town. If this fellow Ritter lives anywhere around Walton, it's even money Arnold's already got a file on him."

Ann stood up and said she'd better be getting home, and they walked slowly to the front door. Instead of opening it, though, he took her in his arms and held her there for a long time. Finally she drew back and said, "Please wait, Alex. I still have so much to do, so many things to decide. I'll call you soon. When it's all right for us to be together."

"I love you," he said. "Only—as you may have guessed—patience isn't really my strong suit."

"I love you, too," she said. "Darling, tell me that's good enough for now?"

He nodded silently, she let herself out, and a few moments later she was speeding away toward Willow Brook Lane.

8

THE FOLLOWING AFTERNOON Carr called the hospital and talked with Lloyd Cunningham. He said he was going to New York on Friday morning and would discuss the idea with his agent.

Cunningham sounded extremely pleased, and immediately said, "Alex, I'll tell you what. When you come back tomorrow afternoon, come over to my place for a drink. I should be there anytime after five. Do say you'll stop by and tell me his reaction, old chap."

Carr agreed, and when he rang off he was smiling to himself. Good news, he thought, for your pal, Ritter. Better give him a call, Lloyd, and tell him you've got that dumb writer completely under your thumb.

And Ritter was still very much on Carr's mind that evening when he met his sister and brother-in-law for dinner at Walton's leading French restaurant, Le Chenonceaux. The question of Ritter's identity could only be discussed, though, after they had disposed of a number of more familiar topics. First Arnold had to be allowed his ritualistic denunciation of greedy and ungrateful clients, and then he and Joyce had to give vent to their mutual anxieties about their two children. Jennifer, aged sixteen and the apple of her father's eye, was still away at a summer tennis camp, and talking more vehemently than ever of a professional tennis career. Dick, soon to commence his junior year at Harvard, was sharing a summer pad in

New York with a couple of his musical chums, the trio joining two or three of their contemporaries in an attempt to gain recognition as a new self-styled rock group, The Something Else.

Coffee already was on the table, and Joyce, guilt-ridden but content, was halfway through a *crème au chocolat*, when Carr decided it was time to bring the name of Ritter into the conversation. "There seem to be three in the phone book," he told Arnold. "George, Henry and Egon. Do you happen to know any of them?"

Arnold's suntanned features broke into a smile. "I know two Ritters quite well," he said. "Taking a stab in the dark—does it have anything to do with Cunningham and that yarn of his?"

"It's more than a yarn," Carr said.

"Really?"

"Without any question."

"And you're going to write a piece on it?"

"Eventually. A couple of articles, or maybe a book. When I've done some more digging."

Joyce looked up from her dessert and sighed. "After everything that Arnold and I said? Honestly, Alex, I think it's such a mistake, getting mixed up with a man like that." She sighed again, and spooned out more of the dark chocolate. "But then, dear, I remember even when we were younger, and I was trying to take mother's and father's place, you rarely showed much good common sense."

She retired placidly to her dessert, and Carr was able to turn back to Arnold. "Which two Ritters do you know?"

Arnold drew on his thin cigar and said, "I know George. He's a counterman at Woolworth's. Got into trouble a couple of years ago for car theft. Still a juvenile at the time, though, and no previous arrests, so the police finally agreed to drop the charges."

"I don't believe it's George," Carr said.

"And Henry Ritter used to work over at the dairy. He's retired now. Must be eighty or eighty-five. He lives with his son and daughter-in-law, I think. As far as I know, he's pretty senile."

"So much for Henry. Which leaves Egon—do you have anything on him?"

Arnold shook his head. "The name means nothing to me."

"Can you ask around?"

"Sure. How important is it? You in a hurry?"

"Not especially," Carr said. "I'd just like to learn a little something about him."

"I'll find out and let you know," Arnold told him.

And then, because Joyce had finished the *crème* and was showing signs of restlessness, they abandoned the subject of Egon Ritter and talked of other things.

FRIDAY'S EXCURSION TO NEW YORK put Carr in a holiday mood. Research trips to the city were a different matter, but since no work was involved in catching a train and having lunch with his agent, Carr always looked forward with anticipation to what usually became a brief but festive occasion.

Not everyone in the business admired Mark Watson. Some editors and fellow agents envied him the money he made from a stable of best-selling authors, and claimed that he had no sensitivity or taste, save for what was egregiously cheap or commercial. Others said that his real talent lay in hiring brilliant young assistants and overworking them until they quit—why else was York and Watson an endless, revolving door for editorial talent?

To Carr, Mark Watson was an agent and a friend. Their special bond was that both of them had been in Vietnam, Carr merely for a year's stint as a reporter in Hue and Saigon, Mark for more than fifty combat missions as a pilot in the marines. Now he walked with a limp, the result of having had the toes of his left foot blown off by a burst of shrapnel.

Carr knew that he himself was regarded as one of the firm's least important clients, and that Mark recognized he might never be anything else. At the same time, he suspected that Mark rarely, if ever, was as candid with the rest of his stable, and that occasionally he enjoyed saying whatever he pleased, knowing that his indiscretions would not be repeated afterward in the enemy camp.

A taxi brought Carr from Penn Station to the Hotel Stanhope, opposite the southern wing of the Metropolitan Museum. The elegant dining room was one of Mark's favorite luncheon spots. As usual, he began by making a careful study of the other diners. Then he declared with satisfaction, "Damn good. Nobody's here—the rest of the filthy pack's sitting around the Baroque or Le Marmiton, backbiting each other to death. 'What a pity—I hear old Sam's deal with Paramount fell through last week.' 'And poor Helen—Book-of-the-Month just turned her down on those *Confessions*—not enough sex in the thing, even for *them*!' The usual, Alex? Gin and tonic?"

Over their chilled crab ravigote, Mark related several of the latest publishing stories, and when the coffee came, Carr told him about Cunningham and the events in Walton. When he'd finished he could see that Mark was favorably impressed. "This time you really might be onto something," he said. "It could make a big splash. Get you out of your comfortable rut, Alex, and into the big time. I always said you could—and should—and this just might do it."

"It's still too early to be sure," Carr said. "When I get the tapes, I'll know a lot more. Actually it depends on how much Cunningham's got, and who and what it leads to.''

Mark nodded. "That's so. It also depends on whether he's right or not about the extent of it. If it's the whole country or just local. Even local, though, could be a pretty good piece. Tell me, what's this Cunningham like?''

"Slippery character,'' Carr said. "Minor league wheeler-dealer. Probably a good idea to count the silver before he leaves.''

"How old a man?''

"Late forties I'd say.''

"Queer? Married? Kids?''

"No kids. Getting a divorce soon.''

"Met the wife?''

"A few times.''

"Good looker?''

"*I* think so.''

"God, I'm glad I still live in New York. These suburban things always end up sounding like 'Peyton Place.' What are your plans? Going to marry her?''

"If I do,'' Carr said, "I'll invite you to the wedding.''

Mark looked at his watch. "First write the book, will you? It helps pay for the champagne.'' He signaled the waiter for the bill, signed it, and apologized for having to leave so early. "I'll get to work on the details of a letter of agreement between you and Cunningham,'' he said. "Give him some sort of percentage of what you'd be likely to get. And if he's as interested in money as you say, he'll probably be able to make a nice piece of change going the lecture route afterward. I guess he's figuring on that. Do the college tour. 'How I exposed XYZ International for Polluting our Bodies and Invading our Sex Glands.' He'll make a mint, besides his share of the book.''

They came out into the heat and sunlight of the

early afternoon, and Mark hailed a cab. While waiting for it to pull up, he said to Carr, "I'm really pleased about this. It could be a great story. Make you an international star, Alex." Then the cab door opened, he hopped awkwardly inside, and sped away.

IT WAS AFTER 1:30 PM and Carr remained in a holiday mood. He could have hurried to the station and caught the early train back to Walton, but he decided instead to enjoy the museum for an hour or two, and then catch the four o'clock train.

He strolled across a hot, airless Fifth Avenue, past the cluster of graceless fountains that had replaced the museum's lovely magnolia trees a dozen years before, then up the stone steps to the museum's air-cooled interior.

A short walk brought him to the new Egyptian wing. Many familiar treasures were there, and numerous additions from the museum's cellars, as well—the immense stone statues, the tiny lapis shawabtis, the bronze cats, the inlaid coffins, the always-sinister mummies in their yards of linen wrappings—all better lighted and more imaginatively displayed than previously, but all still as mysterious and romantic as they had been in their darker and less elegant former home. Happily lost in thoughts of the ancient past, he wandered through seemingly endless rooms and corridors, the only sound an occasional footfall on the stone floors.

When it was three-thirty he tore himself away, trotted down the museum steps and hailed a cab. He caught the four o'clock train with three minutes to spare, and after dozing for most of the journey, arrived at the Walton station just before five.

The air still was warm but not oppressive as he

drove the Volkswagen out of the station parking lot and down Route 23 toward Willow Brook Lane. He felt sleepy and content, and wondered whether he ought to accept a second drink if Cunningham should offer it. He also wondered, not for the first time, whether Cunningham had mentioned his coming over, and what chance there was that Ann might also be there.

Behind him he heard the rising wail of a siren and, slowing down the Volkswagen, drew nearer to the edge of the road. A moment later an ambulance flashed by, one of the pair maintained by Walton's Emergency and Rescue Service. The ambulance disappeared around the next curve and before long the sound of the siren died out, as well.

A few minutes later Carr turned left, off the blacktop road, and drove the last quarter of a mile to Willow Brook Lane. It was then that he saw the ambulance again. It was parked in the driveway of the Cunningham's house, the rear door standing open.

He parked out front and walked up the narrow driveway toward the house. After a few yards he had to stop and draw aside. Two attendants were carrying a stretcher back to the ambulance. Behind them walked a young doctor, the ends of his stethoscope dangling from a pocket in his short white jacket. On the stretcher Carr saw the body of a tall man, covered from crown to ankles by a hospital blanket.

"What happened?" Carr asked as they went by.

"Heart failure," the doctor said. "It's always a risk when you're in Mr. Cunningham's condition."

"Nothing you could do for him?"

"No, we were much too late. Are you a friend of his?"

"Yes. And a business associate."

The doctor paused. "Do you think you could tell the family? His wife isn't home."

Carr said he would tell Mrs. Cunningham, whenever she got back, and then stood aside and watched the attendants turn the stretcher, so that they could place it inside the ambulance. He was vaguely aware that a thin, gray-haired woman had come from the direction of the house and was standing beside him. She had a sharp, birdlike face, and peered intently at the attendants and their burden.

"Did you come over to see the Cunninghams?" she asked Carr.

"Yes. I had an appointment with Lloyd."

"I was the one who called the ambulance," she told him. "I live next door. I'm Adele Nichols. I was the one who found him."

The two attendants had finished turning the stretcher and now they lifted it headfirst into the back of the ambulance. Cunningham's feet extended from under the blanket. Two huge feet, encased in an equally huge pair of worn brown shoes. In the sole of one, Carr saw, there was a round hole the size of a silver dollar. The kind of hole that a man might have in his shoe if he was desperately poor, or if he had a wife who no longer cared very much about his appearance.

Then the door of the ambulance shut, and that was the last time he saw Lloyd Cunningham, architect of complex and dubious schemes, who so recently had dreamed of turning the entire country upside down.

9

AFTER THE AMBULANCE HAD DISAPPEARED down Willow Brook Lane, Carr asked Mrs. Nichols if she knew where her neighbor might be, and was informed that Ann Cunningham had left for the city sometime before noon, having received an important call from the New York gallery that handled her work.

"Did she tell you what train she'd be taking back?" Carr said.

"The five o'clock, if she could make it. She said it would still get her home...in time to fix Lloyd his supper."

Carr glanced at his watch and said, "It's after six already. I think I'll wait for her at the house."

He turned and started up the driveway and Mrs. Nichols came pattering nervously after him. Reaching the back of the house, Carr saw a canvas deck chair on the patio, and the garden sprinkler slowly revolving in the middle of the lawn. Without thinking he went over to the side of the house and turned off the water, and when he returned Mrs. Nichols said, "The sprinkler was going when I came over, and Lloyd was lying in the chair, right out in the sun. He'd been there a long time, and I was afraid he'd fallen asleep and would get a bad burn. But when I tried to wake him up I couldn't, and then I saw how his face looked sort of blotchy and his lips were blue, and I remembered about his heart. So I ran back to our house as quick as I could and called the Emergency Service."

There was a strain of hysteria in her voice, and Carr wondered if a drink might help to calm her, but decided it would be better simply to let her talk out her feelings.

"It must have been a terrible shock for you," he said.

Mrs. Nichols's small, birdlike head bobbed up and down. "Yes, it certainly was—finding him that way. Most times, of course, I wouldn't even have noticed him out there in the sun. But before she went this morning Ann asked me to keep an eye on the house, because she was expecting some art supplies today and wanted to make sure the package was delivered all right."

"It was very lucky you did notice," Carr said. "Otherwise Ann might have come home and found the...ambulance still here."

Mrs. Nichols nodded again. "Yes, that would have been worse, wouldn't it? But I've been watching on and off all day, and that's why I noticed Lloyd out in his chair. It really did keep me busy, looking over here the way she asked. First it was a man from the ABC company, bringing them a tank of water softener, and after the ABC man there was someone from the Environmental Agency to see about some kind of bug infestation that's been spreading all over. But no parcel delivery with her package—though I don't suppose that's going to matter much to poor Ann now."

She glanced uneasily at Carr and said, "I really ought to be getting back home pretty soon. I have to fix supper, too. Will you stay awhile...and tell her? I'll come back later and make sure she's all right."

He said he would tell Ann, and then watched Adele Nichols scurry eagerly for home. A few minutes later he heard a car being parked in the street and, returning to the front, met Ann as she came striding toward the house.

At first she scarcely seemed aware of him, or of the fact that he was standing in the driveway, blocking her path. Her fists were clenched, her body tense with anger. "Somebody's going to pay for this," she said. "The damn bitch—or maybe it was her husband. Imagine—yesterday afternoon they were at the gallery, loved my work, wanted at least two things, maybe more. Could I meet them today and help them choose? So, in I went—and they never showed up. The hotel said they'd checked out, left no messages, no forwarding address. A marvelous practical joke. So funny. First get the gallery people all worked up, and then have me waste the entire day, riding back and forth on that goddamned hot dirty train!"

The outburst over, she looked at Carr and only then seemed to realize fully that he was there. She smiled and said, "Oh—I didn't know you were coming over today. What a nice surprise."

When he didn't answer, her smile faded. She stared at him and glanced beyond his shoulder in the direction of the house. Finally she said, "Where's Lloyd now? Did you have an appointment and get here early? Alex—why are you standing there like that? Something's the matter, I can tell it is."

He guided her up to the house and into the kitchen and, as gently as he could, explained what had happened while she'd been away. Then he poured some whiskey into a glass and put it in front of her on the kitchen table.

"Christ," she said, "Oh, Christ, poor Lloyd. What an awful thing. If only I'd been here, maybe I could have helped him."

"I really don't think there was anything you could have done," Carr said.

"But if only *someone* had been here. Don't you see? It's so much worse that it happened when he was alone."

He edged the whiskey toward her, and after she drank some the color gradually returned to her face. When he was sure she was calmer he began to point out some of the practical steps that would have to be taken during the next few days, and offered to help in any way he could.

She thanked him, but insisted that she would take charge of whatever arrangements were necessary. "Until after all this is over," she said, "you really mustn't try to do anything for me. You don't know this town the way I do. People around here love nothing better than to gossip, and since nobody knew that Lloyd and I were planning to get a divorce, can't you imagine how tongues would wag if they saw you hovering over the bereaved widow, even before her husband had been decently buried?"

"There are so many things, though, that have to be taken care of," he said. "I've been through it myself. That's why I hate to see you entirely on your own."

"But I won't be," she said. "Your brother-in-law was Lloyd's lawyer, so I can call him now, and he'll be able to tell me what to do. And then I'll talk with Lloyd's brother, and make whatever arrangements suit him and the rest of the family. Really, Alex, between them both, I'll have all the help I'll need."

"I don't like the idea of your being alone," he said. "Could you stay somewhere else—or have a friend come over here for a couple of days?"

"I'll be all right by myself," she said.

"It can be awful rough at first. Look, there's an extra bedroom at my place—completely private, with a separate bathroom, just like having your own suite at a hotel. If you'd like...."

She shook her head. "No, Alex, when I come over to spend the night at Purley's Cottage, it won't be like that. I'll pack a toothbrush and my prettiest nightgown, and I'll sleep with you in the master bedroom—after we've both decided it's time for us to start sleeping there."

He knew she was right and that for the time being he had no useful place in her affairs. She did promise that if there was any serious trouble she would call him at once, and then he drove home and prepared to endure the next few days as well as he could.

She called him each evening after that, and told him what she had done during the day, and he also learned from Arnold Daniels what arrangements were being made for the approaching funeral. On Sunday morning Carr attended a small private service in the hospital chapel, where he saw Ann briefly and exchanged a few words. Then on Monday she left for upstate New York with her brother-in-law, and the next day, a second service was held with Lloyd Cunningham's numerous relatives in attendance.

IN WALTON on the same Tuesday afternoon a curious thing occurred at Purley's Cottage. Carr had driven into town to buy some groceries, and on the way home a package had fallen off the seat, spilling a half dozen oranges across the floor. After parking near the shed, Carr leaned over to retrieve them. One of the oranges had rolled into a corner under the glove compartment so that to reach it, he first had to stretch out at full length on the seat. As he picked up the orange he glanced at the underside of the dashboard and saw a small round object attached to it. He got out, went inside the kitchen and, after putting away the groceries, returned to the car again. Bending over, he felt the metal object with the tips of his fingers. Then he gave it a firm tug, and a moment later it came away in his hand.

He lifted it out and carried it into the garden and stared at it for a while without moving. He couldn't be sure that he'd ever seen a similar object before, except possibly in a photograph, yet he felt certain that he knew what it was. And he also knew that somebody had waited until his car was unattended, and then had hidden it under the dashboard in order to overhear whatever he might say to anyone riding with him.

Finally he slipped the metal disc into his pocket, returned to the cottage and picked up the phone. His brother-in-law was in his office, and Carr said, "I've come across a little problem here, Arnold. I'm going to the borough police with it. Who's the best man to see there?"

"John McGill. He's an ex-New York detective. Came here after he retired, about five or six years ago. I'd say he's honest and savvy, and knows his way around." Arnold paused. Then he said, "What kind of trouble is it, Alex?"

"I just found a bug in my car."

"Really? Any idea who put it there?"

"No."

"I hate to speak ill of the dead, but what about Cunningham?"

"Anything's possible. I'd put him on the list."

He heard Arnold sigh heavily. "Well, I'm not really surprised—I tried to warn you about him. Anyway, I've been meaning to call, because I've finally picked up something on your man Ritter."

"Oh?"

"Works for the A. and S. Chemical Company. They've got a plant a couple of miles from here, on

the east side of town. Ritter came here about seven
or eight years ago, but I don't know where he was
before that, or what he was doing. I haven't been
able to find out yet.''

"Every little bit helps," Carr said.

"Has Ritter got much to do with the stuff Cunningham was digging up?"

"Probably a good deal. I'm not sure, though. So let
me know if you learn any more.''

"I will, Alex. And give me a ring after you've
talked with the lieutenant. I'll be interested to hear
what he's got to say.''

Carr promised to call that night, and after hanging
up, returned to the shed and once more drove into
Walton.

THE BOROUGH POLICE had its headquarters in a squat
two-story stucco building several blocks beyond Mc-
Carter Square, on the way to Walton Hospital. Two
blue squad cars were parked at the curb and a uni-
formed officer was standing by the front entrance,
out of the bright July sun. Carr asked for Lieutenant
McGill, and was shown to a small rectangular air-
conditioned office at the back of the building.

A few minutes later the lieutenant came in from
the hall, a wiry gray-haired man in a rumpled pair
of brown slacks and a short-sleeved white shirt. He
put out his hand and said, "Two refugees from New
York—glad to meet you, Mr. Carr. Please have a
seat. I already feel that I know something about
you. From my wife, Helen, at the library. She told
me you'd been a big help to them last month, setting
up the fair. And you'd made a speech at one of their
other fund-raisers—Celebrity Night, I think they call
it.''

"Quite a dossier you've got on me," Carr said
with a grin.

"I guess people don't change a lot," the lieutenant told him. "Back in the city, when I was starting out as a cop on the beat, I tried to know everybody in my neighborhood. Sometimes it came in handy, so I figured the same thing might apply here in Walton. Smoke? I wish I could kick the habit myself. Now—tell me what brings you here, and what I can do for you?"

Carr slid the small metal disc across the desk and watched the lieutenant pick it up and turn it over in his hand. At the same time the open cordial expression in his gray eyes changed to a look of sharp interest. "Do you know what this is, Mr. Carr?"

"I believe so. Some sort of bug, isn't it?"

"That's right. Quite a good one, too. Interestingly enough, I'd say it's a foreign model, and you don't see many of them around. Mind if I ask where you got it?"

"Under the dashboard of my car."

The lieutenant whistled softly. "Someone bugging you? Any notion who?"

Carr shook his head. "No, I can't say I have."

"Interesting." The lieutenant continued to examine the bug for several minutes, and then he said, "I wonder if you'd mind showing me just where you found it?"

They went outside into the summer heat and Lieutenant McGill opened the front door of the car and peered under the dashboard. Then he said, "No objections if I look around?" and without waiting for permission, climbed inside and began to examine everything from the car roof to the floorboards.

A moment later he whistled again. He asked Carr if he had a screwdriver in his tool kit, and then took a handkerchief out of his pants pocket and put it over the end of one of the door handles. After Carr handed him the screwdriver, he twisted it several times, removed the door handle, and wrapped it inside the handkerchief. Finally he climbed out of the Volkswagen and slammed the door.

Carr followed him back inside the office. The lieutenant placed his handkerchief on the desk, and then said to Carr, "You can take a look if you want, but please don't touch. It's a hundred to one there's nothing on it, but I'll try to pick up a print. Do you know what this is—right here—this little piece of metal inside the handle?"

"I've no idea," Carr said.

The lieutenant's expression was wary and reserved. "The one you found was fairly run-of-the-mill, but this model's the latest thing in the line. It's damn sophisticated. *And* expensive."

"A second bug?" Carr said blankly.

"That's right. Obviously somebody else wants to keep tabs on you, and they know exactly how to go about doing it. This one's a first-rate professional job. Real big-league stuff. Can you think of any reason why an expert would want to be doing this to you?"

"Well, I've started working on a new project," Carr said. "Maybe somebody's suddenly got interested in me."

"And who might that somebody be?"

"I really don't know," Carr said. "And if I did, I'm not at all sure I could tell you."

"What sort of project is it?"

"At the moment, Lieutenant, it's got to stay confidential. Among other things, I have to protect my sources."

"Well, suit yourself," the lieutenant said. "But if you don't mind, I'll give you a piece of advice. I don't know who you've been keeping company with, Mr. Carr, but I'd say for certain it's a pretty fast crowd. Think about it for a day or two, and then maybe you'll change your mind and come in again and we can have another talk."

The lieutenant stood up and put out his hand. "I'm suggesting you do that," he said, "because I think you're in deeper water than you realize. To put the matter bluntly, Mr. Carr, if I were in *your* shoes, I wouldn't be worrying about protecting my sources—I'd be paying up my life insurance and looking for a good place to hide."

10

EARLY IN THE AFTERNOON on the day following the funeral. Carr drove over to the house on Willow Brook Lane. He found Ann Cunningham in the living room, staring glumly at the pile of condolence letters she'd received from Lloyd's colleagues at Walton Hospital.

She left no doubt about her feelings, opening her arms and giving him a kiss that was warm and lingering. "Christ, Alex, I made an awful mistake," she said at last. "I never should have gone up there alone."

"Had a bad time in the provinces?"

"Terrible. Lloyd's brother's the most pompous ass in the world. And the Cunningham cousins aren't a whole lot better."

After a while they drew apart and looked down at the pile of letters lying on the coffee table. Ann said she'd have to try to answer them later, and then they went outside and sat together on the patio. The sky was hazy and the air at the back of the house warm and humid. She described her trip in more detail, and when she'd finished Carr told her about the two bugs that had been found in the Volkswagen the previous day, and what Lieutenant McGill had thought about them.

"I guess whatever Lloyd was up to," she said, "he's got you involved in it, too."

"One way or another," Carr agreed. He stood up

and looked around the patio, wondering why he felt ill at ease. Then he saw the canvas deck chair by the edge of the grass, and remembered that on the previous Friday afternoon Lloyd Cunningham's body had been stretched out in it.

"I'll put this away," he told Ann and, folding up the chair, placed it in a less conspicuous position against the side of the house.

After he came back and sat down, though, he still felt a vague sense of uneasiness. An idea was troubling him, teasing at a remote corner of his mind—something he had either heard or seen without being consciously aware of it.

"What's the matter, Alex?" she finally said. "You haven't been listening at all."

He said that something was puzzling him and, rising again, slowly began to circle the patio. His glance wandered over to the house next door, and then back across the lawn, in the opposite direction. He looked at the hazy sky, the bushes under the dining-room windows, and back to Mrs. Nichols's house again.

The second time around, it struck him.

He didn't know its significance, only that what his eye had noticed didn't make any sense whatever. "Please come over here," he said, "and take a look at this."

Ann crossed to the edge of the patio and he pointed to the center of the lawn, where the garden sprinkler stood. It still occupied the same position it had on Friday afternoon when he'd found it running and had turned the water off. Now, though, a change had occurred. While the rest of the lawn looked high and green, in perfect condition, around the sprinkler the grass was dead and eaten away, leaving an irregular circle of naked, brown earth.

They walked over and examined the bare ground,

which, on closer inspection, proved to be encrusted with a few thin patches of chalky white powder.

"The sprinkler must have been left on too long," she said, "and the water killed the grass."

Carr shook his head. "Water alone never did that," he told her. "Your grass was killed by acid, or some kind of solvent."

He stooped down and poked at one of the chalky patches. A few particles clung to his finger and he stuck out his tongue and touched them gingerly. "It's salt," he said. "Or maybe something a little stronger."

When they were back on the patio again, Carr said, "The sprinkler was running on Friday afternoon—I saw that myself. Something, though, had been put in the water—probably salt, or some kind of sodium compound. Only for the life of me, I can't imagine why Lloyd would have wanted to run salt or acid through his garden sprinkler. . . ."

"It doesn't make any sense," she said. "Why would he do such a thing?"

"Or maybe it wasn't Lloyd who turned the sprinkler on. Maybe it was somebody else—*after* Lloyd was dead. Somebody who already had put something into the water pipes, and then had to flush it out with acid or a solvent."

Carr slowly removed his glasses and stuck them carelessly into his shirt pocket. Then he shut his eyes and covered them with his hands, as he sometimes did when he was trying to concentrate.

"Just give me a minute to think," he said. "I've already got the start of it. My God, though, if I'm right, Ann, we've really been asleep."

After a time he lifted his head and absently reached for his glasses again. "I believe I've worked out most of it," he told her. "Friday afternoon, when I got here, I naturally assumed that Lloyd had turned on the sprinkler to water the lawn, and that afterward he'd had a heart attack, and the sprinkler simply kept on running. But that isn't the way it happened. Because we've forgotten a number of other things—the most important being that you weren't here on Friday."

"I certainly wasn't," she said.

"But *why*?"

"Because some lousy practical joker had me waste an entire day chasing back and forth to New York. Whenever I think of those sons of bitches, I get so mad I could just about scream."

Carr looked at the burned out patch on the lawn, then at the folded deck chair, and finally back at the dark-haired woman seated near him on the patio. "I don't believe there were any practical jokers," he said. "The people who had you go up there on Friday weren't playing a silly game. They wanted to get you away from here, and they wanted to make sure you wouldn't come back all day."

"But why, Alex?"

"So that Lloyd could be killed, and his death made to look completely natural."

"Killed? But how—and for what reason?"

"We aren't likely to know the reason," he said, "until we can get into Lloyd's safe-deposit box and listen to the tapes he made. Unfortunately, the bank must have sealed the box by now—they always do after somebody dies—so we won't be able to hear the tapes for a while. But the way Lloyd was killed isn't too hard to figure out. I think I already know how they must have worked it, only just to be sure, I'd like to ask Mrs. Nichols a question or two—do you think we could go over there now and see if she's in?"

They walked over to the house next door and found Adele Nichols in her kitchen, reading the day's papers. She insisted on making fresh coffee and serving them sponge cake and a coffee ring, and while she was bustling about preparing things, Roland, her ancient Saint Bernard, finally roused himself from his afternoon stupor. He sniffed at the new arrivals, and apparently decided that he preferred male companionship, for without warning he placed his huge head on Carr's lap, and began to drool incontinently on the leg of his trousers.

When Roland had been noisily exiled to the yard, a number of apologies had been made, and the coffee and cake were on the table, Carr said to Mrs. Nichols, "I know it's upsetting to think about last Friday, but Ann has a little problem, and I suggested that you might be able to help her with it."

"I'd be glad to do anything I can," Mrs. Nichols said.

"Well, you see, Ann isn't sure, but she has an idea that a couple of things might be missing from the house and the garage. So we thought if we knew exactly who came here when she was away, and while Lloyd was here, too, it might clarify the problem and ease her mind a bit. Might we ask you just a few questions about what happened here on Friday?"

Mrs. Nichols indicated that she had no objections, and so Carr said, "As I understand it, Ann came over around ten to say she was going to catch the 10:55 train to New York, and would you keep an eye out for the package of art supplies she was expecting?"

"That's right," Mrs. Nichols said.

"And then you saw this man from the ABC Company, bringing in a new tank of water softener for the Cunninghams? About when was that?"

"Only a couple of minutes after Ann left. Maybe ten-fifteen."

"On Friday," Carr said, "I think you told me about

a man from the Environmental Agency. Did he come by before Lloyd got back from the hospital?"

"Oh, yes, long before," Mrs. Nichols said.

"And he stopped here at your house?"

"That's right. He wanted to know how many families lived along the Lane, and if there was anyone home next door, and I told him no, that both Lloyd and you were away, Ann."

"Did he say what he wanted?"

"Yes, he showed me his identification card, and told me the agency—the Environmental Protection Agency, he called it—was very much concerned about the Gypsy moth infestation. It was spreading south from New York State and New England, and he was going to spend some time around here, checking on all our trees and bushes. Such a fine looking man, too. Do either of you remember the old Andy Hardy movies, years ago? The ones with Mickey Rooney and his father, the white-haired judge? Well, that's exactly what Mr. Englehardt reminded me of—wise, kindly Judge Hardy in the movies."

"And what happened," Ann said, "after Mr. Englehardt went off to look at our trees?"

Mrs. Nichols thought for a moment, and then she said, "Well, as far as I can remember, dear, Lloyd must have come home after that, because I saw him out back, moving his chair around on the patio."

"What time was that?" Carr said.

"Maybe three or three-thirty. He sat on the chair, and drank something from his glass, and then he put the glass down on that little patio table of yours, Ann, and just stretched out full length and seemed to go to sleep."

"Did you happen to notice," Carr said, "if the sprinkler was on?"

Mrs. Nichols frowned. "Later it was," she said.

"So I guess it must have been on by then—but I can't say for sure, because I don't remember seeing it."

"And then," Ann asked her, "what happened after that?"

"Well, I went inside and made the beds, so I didn't notice much else for the next half hour or so. Except that I did keep an eye on your driveway, of course, so I know that your package didn't come."

"And while you were making the beds," Carr said, "did you happen to see the ABC man again?"

Mrs. Nichols glanced at him with surprise and a trace of suspicion, swallowed some coffee, and scratched her head. "You know, that's a funny thing," she said. "In the excitement and all, I'd forgotten—but I did see the ABC man again from the bedroom window, just after I'd been changing the sheets."

"What was he doing?" Carr said.

"Carrying a tank back to his panel truck. In fact, now that I remember, he did that twice—carried one tank down, then came back to your garage, Ann, and carried down a second tank, too. A couple of minutes later I heard him drive away, and I didn't think any more about him."

"And after that?" Ann said.

"After that, dear, I saw Lloyd out in the sun—asleep I thought—and so I came over to your house, because I was afraid he'd get a bad burn if he didn't wake up."

"Well, we don't need to bother you any more," Carr said quickly. "And we want to thank you for being so patient. I'm sure it's going to help Ann find what she's looking for."

They finished their coffee and cake, thanked Mrs. Nichols a second time, and then went back next door. When they were seated on the patio again, Carr said, "It seems pretty clear what happened, doesn't it? There were two of them—one togged out as an ABC man, and the other posing as an agent from the E.P.A. Shall I tell you how I think they set Lloyd up?''

She nodded and Carr said, ''When they were sure you had left for the train, Ann, one of them must have telephoned Lloyd at the hospital and scheduled an appointment to see him here, between three and four. At the same time, knowing the coast was clear, the ABC man arrived and carried his two tanks up to your garage. He disconnected your regular tank of water softener, and connected the first replacement—the one loaded with whatever they used to kill Lloyd. Once he'd done that, he simply stored the second replacement tank in a handy corner—the tank filled with the salt solution they had to use afterward—went back to the panel truck, and drove away.

''Before long, Englehardt arrived—whoever he is; maybe he's Ritter—to check on how his plan was working. At any rate, Lloyd came home for his appointment—perhaps thinking he was going to meet Ritter, or someone important that Ritter had promised to bring along, or maybe to meet an entirely different party. Lloyd ran some water in the kitchen, carried his glass outside here, fixed up his chair to have a short rest before his appointment, and swallowed the water and one of his pills. The water, of course, was doctored with something, quite possibly with a high concentration of digoxin, which would produce the symptoms of a heart attack for the doctor who'd come later—and the poison killed him within a minute or so.

''After that, Englehardt, who was keeping an eye on things, must have come over here to the house, made certain Lloyd was dead, and pocketed the incriminating water glass—which you remember we didn't find here afterward. He would also have to go to the garage—it would only take a couple of minutes—disconnect the poison tank, hook up the tank with the salt solution, and then turn on the sprinkler full blast to drain off the poison that was still in the pipes. Most likely he also went into the kitchen for a moment and ran salt water out of the faucet, so that your kitchen pipes would be completely cleansed and drained, too. Then he only had to go to a phone somewhere, call the ABC man, and tell him to return in an hour or so to pick up the two tanks they'd used. By that time, enough of the solvent would have run through the sprinkler so that any trace of the poison would be gone, and when you returned from your trip to the city, the water in your house would be perfectly safe to drink again."

"That was certainly thoughtful of them," she said. "I'm touched that they were so concerned about my safety."

"It wasn't your safety that really mattered," Carr said. "They just didn't want anyone else to have a heart attack and die in the house a couple of hours after Lloyd did. It would have blown the whole 'accidental death' game sky-high."

"So I had to be kept out of the way on Friday," she said. "Two bodies would have been one too many."

"I'm afraid that's about it."

"But are you really sure of all this, Alex? How can you prove they murdered Lloyd the way you've said?"

"Why not call up the ABC people? Mrs. Nichols saw the man here. Call them up now, and ask them if they delivered a fresh tank to your house on Friday?"

Ann went inside to the kitchen, and for several minutes he heard her speaking on the phone. When she came back he said, "What did they tell you?"

"They said they hadn't made a delivery here last Friday. They looked it up in their books and said we're not due for a new tank for another two weeks. I talked with the dispatcher, and then with the district manager. No ABC man was here on Friday—morning or afternoon."

Then she sat down and said, "What are we going to do? Those two men murdered Lloyd—we've got to find out who they are, and then turn them over to the police."

"Look, Ann, there's something you ought to know about me," Carr said. "I'm not too strong on the personal heroism stuff. In the movies it works out fine, of course. The hero gets into a mess, decides to go it alone, and after making a complete hash out of things until the last reel—and nearly getting himself and everybody else killed off in the process—finally unmasks the villains, untangles the plot and goes off into the sunset with his sweetie, to live happily ever after.

"Only I learned a long time ago that life and the movies aren't quite the same proposition. So I'm not going to find out who killed Lloyd—it's not the kind of thing I'd be likely to do very well, anyway. Instead, we'll take my car now and drive down to the local police, tell Lieutenant McGill what I think happened here, and then let the professionals handle it anyway they like."

"But Alex, there's really so little evidence. Except for Mrs. Nichols, what is there?"

"The lieutenant," Carr said, "can collect all the evidence he needs. He can get a court order and have Lloyd's body exhumed. When they've done an autopsy I have no doubt the authorities will find that he was killed by a large dose of digoxin, or a similar drug."

"And in the meantime, we're to do nothing?"

"That's the idea," Carr said. "We'll give them the facts, and then the police will find out who murdered Lloyd and why. That's their job, and I'm sure they'll do it promptly and efficiently."

And the curious thing was it sounded like the sensible thing to do—at least it sounded that way out on the patio at the time when he said it.

11

LIEUTENANT MCGILL RECEIVED THEM at borough headquarters with an expression of polite interest and arranged two chairs for them near his desk. He offered his sympathy to Ann on the recent death of her husband, and then, after a speculative glance at Carr, asked what had prompted them to visit his office.

The lieutenant's gray eyes strayed back and forth between them, as he listened to Ann's explanation—her brief description of the physical circumstances surrounding Lloyd Cunningham's death, Carr's noticing the unusual condition of the lawn, their visit to her neighbor, Mrs. Nichols, and finally her own telephone call to the ABC Company.

When she'd finished, the lieutenant leaned forward on his desk and said with a quizzical smile, "Then if I understand what you've been telling me, Mrs. Cunningham, you first believed—naturally enough—that your husband had died of a heart attack. But now you no longer believe so. In point of fact, you think he was killed deliberately by two men who came to your house on the day he died."

"It looks suspiciously like it," Ann said.

"And Mr. Carr agrees with you?"

"Completely."

The lieutenant paused to rub his chin. Then he said, "Do you have any idea who the two men might have been? Did Mrs. Nichols's description of the man from the E.P.A., Mr. Englehardt, suggest anyone you know? A friend, an acquaintance? A professional associate of Mr. Cunningham's?"

Ann shook her head. "No, I have no idea who either of the men were."

"Or the reason why two strangers should have wanted to kill your husband?"

"I have no proof," she said, "but I believe—Alex and I are quite certain, in fact—that it must have had something to do with what Lloyd discovered at the hospital a number of weeks ago."

"And what did he discover?"

"Something he called the Amazon Factor," Carr told the lieutenant. "Thanks to a chance remark by one of the hospital nurses, Lloyd discovered that for the past year or so the birth rate here in Walton has been wildly out of balance—an excess of infant girls, a shortage of infant boys."

"Something he called the Amazon Factor?" the lieutenant said. "Surely there must have been more to it than that?" He paused, and then, seemingly as an afterthought, he added, "Are you concerned in all of this, Mr. Carr, simply as a friend of the family—or does your interest in Lloyd Cunningham's death have some connection with the problem we've already discussed?"

"There's a very close connection," Carr said.

The lieutenant turned to Ann. "Mr. Carr came to see me yesterday, after he found that someone had placed a listening device in his Volkswagen. I examined his car, and found a second bug inside. I said I thought he was getting into pretty deep water—perhaps he mentioned it to you?"

"Yes, he told me about it," Ann said.

Carr found the lieutenant eyeing him again. "And did Mr. Cunningham's discovery have anything to do with the source you were protecting?"

"It did," Carr said. "I'd agreed to work with Lloyd—to write some articles or a book about the story he'd stumbled across, if we could draw up a satisfactory agreement. At the time when I saw you, I thought it would be best to keep the matter as confidential as possible—to keep it out of the papers if I could—in order to protect my own professional interests."

"But now you feel you can talk more freely?"

"After what's happened," Carr said, "I see no reason to hold anything back."

The lieutenant nodded, withdrew a pad from his desk and indicated that he was ready to listen, and Carr began to describe how Lloyd Cunningham had first approached him, and all that had transpired since then.

When the recital was over, Carr saw the lieutenant push aside his pad and frown. "Well, I must admit it's interesting," he said. "Or I should say, it's different." Then he stood up, excused himself, and left the room. A few moments later he returned, a newspaper in one hand, a large glass of water in the other. He opened his desk drawer, took out a bottle of pills and, with a surprisingly fussy gesture, gulped several of them down in rapid succession.

"Vitamin C," he explained between swallows. "My wife, Helen, put me on to it. Surefire protection—now I never get a summer cold. I haven't had one in years."

He sat down at his desk again and for a minute or two said nothing at all. Finally he looked up and shook his head. "Back in New York, the first year I was on the detective squad, I worked for a very smart man. Detective Lieutenant Alvin Rosenberg. 'McGill,' he used to say to me, 'above everything else a detective needs a good nose. That way he'll know when something's fishy, even if he can't see who's hiding the fish.' "

"And your nose," Carr said, "isn't too happy with what we've been telling you?"

"That's right. Yesterday I didn't like the bugs in your car. And today, I don't like the rest of the setup any better."

The lieutenant shrugged. "But I'm only a public servant, and my likes and dislikes don't count for much, do they? You're the taxpayers here, and you have an important matter you'd like me to investigate. The trouble is, what you've given me so far is only guesswork. Suspicion of murder, based on a couple of hunches. From the official point of view it's pretty flimsy stuff to go ahead with."

"But you *are* going to look into my husband's death, aren't you?" Ann said, and Carr was surprised to see her impatient frown, and to hear the anger in her voice. "I mean, Lieutenant," she went on quickly, "you almost sound as though you're sorry we came."

The lieutenant shrugged again. "Sorry or not, Mrs. Cunningham, you *have* come, which gives me no choice but to try and learn what's really happened."

He stood up slowly, walked to the window and peered out at the summer sky. "As a matter of fact," he said, "I've already started to work—just now, when I was outside, I read the latest weather report. It's been pretty dry since the day your husband died, but tonight there's a ninety-percent chance of rain. So now I'll want to run over to your house and have a look at the lawn—before whatever's there gets washed away."

THE LIEUTENANT USHERED THEM OUT to the front of the building, and as they approached the red Volkswagen, he said to Ann, "I'd like to follow you home in one of our unmarked vehicles, Mrs. Cunningham.

A police car always attracts attention. No sense in stir-
ring up your neighbors any more than we have to."

Carr waited until the lieutenant had got behind the
wheel of a dark coupe, and then he started up the
Volkswagen and drove slowly away from the headquarters building. Ann remained silent, and after a
minute or two Carr looked at her and said, "I guess
you're browned off about something—what's on
your mind?"

"I was only thinking that I don't actually care a
whole lot for your Lieutenant McGill."

"So I imagined. In fact, at one point back there, I
was afraid you were going to give him a lecture on
the proper way to handle a police case."

"Well, I think he deserved a lecture. I mean, he
began to annoy me, with all his foot dragging and his
lame excuses."

"He was just stalling for time," Carr said. "So that
he could figure out how things stood, and what to do
first."

"And besides, I didn't like his macho attitude toward me."

"His *what*?"

"Alex, he was very condescending. The way he
talked to me. As if I were simply a dumb, hysterical,
addlepated female who'd only come there to annoy
him and waste his valuable time."

"Did you really feel that? I thought he took what
we had to say quite seriously."

"Naturally you thought so—he was different with
you, love. Just two good-old-boys, chatting together,
both on the same sensible, masculine wavelength.
But he didn't talk to me like that, and when I finally
noticed the difference, I got very irritated and simply
let it show, that's all."

Carr grinned and said, "You do have a pretty short
fuse, don't you?"

"Of course. I'm quick to anger, and I'm just as quick to cool off. I thought you already knew that."

"Not until now," Carr said. "I guess we still have a few things to learn about each other."

"Yes," Ann said, "at least a few."

There was another spell of silence, and then she shifted around on the seat to study him. "What was Eve like?" she finally said. "Did she have a good disposition, or was she hot-tempered like me?"

"Most of the time she was pretty easygoing."

"But once in a while she really blew her stack?"

"Well, now and again. I remember one night we were going to a fancy party, and the dress she planned to wear was over at the cleaners. I'd promised to pick it up so she could stay at the office longer, but I forgot, so she had to go to the party wearing something else. God, was I in the doghouse for a while."

"I'm surprised she ever let you out," Ann said.

"The passage of time, I suppose. And my irresistible charm."

"There was that, of course."

"You'll find out for yourself some day. And despite your better judgment, forgive me for my innumerable sins."

She laughed softly and said, "If I were you, darling, I wouldn't count on it. I'm not the forgiving type." Then she leaned toward him, slid an arm around his waist and, holding him close, began to kiss him on the side of the neck, until he reminded her that her friend Lieutenant McGill was in the car directly behind them, with what was no doubt an unobstructed view of their current activities.

A FEW MINUTES LATER they turned into Willow Brook Lane and parked in front of the house, and before long the dark coupe had drawn up and parked behind them. After climbing out, the lieutenant opened the trunk of the coupe and withdrew a blue canvas traveling bag. Then they led him around to the patio, pointed out the Nichols's house, and showed him the position the beach chair had occupied on the afternoon Mrs. Nichols had come over and found Lloyd Cunningham's body.

From the patio they walked across the lawn as far as the circle of brown earth where the sprinkler had stood that afternoon. When he saw the ruined grass the lieutenant whistled softly and set his bag down on the ground. Opening the bag, he drew out several small manila envelopes and began to fill them with samples of earth, grass and white powder, carefully labeling each envelope before putting it aside. Then he placed a pinch of the white powder on his tongue and, after a moment, informed them that it was either salt or some other kind of solvent.

After reassembling the envelopes and returning them to the canvas bag, the lieutenant produced a Polaroid camera and began to take pictures of the damaged lawn from a variety of angles. He'd already snapped a dozen pictures, when he paused for a moment, and said without looking up, "We're about to have a visitor."

A moment later Adele Nichols joined them. She said hello to Ann and Carr and asked them how they were, before turning her attention to the squatting policeman.

"Why, Lieutenant McGill, what a pleasant surprise," she said. "I haven't seen you since the Fourth of July at the fireworks display."

The lieutenant murmured something about the unexpected pleasure of seeing Mrs. Nichols again, and snapped another picture. Ann's neighbor glanced furtively at the patch of bare earth, and then eyed the lieutenant and his camera. Finally, her expression an uneasy blend of curiosity and apprehension, she said to Ann, "I hope everything's all right, dear. There isn't any trouble, is there?"

"It's nothing to worry about," the lieutenant broke in, as he closed his camera and rose to his feet. "I just came over to have a look at Mrs. Cunningham's lawn. Possibility of vandalism—not very much damage, though."

Mrs. Nichols allowed herself a second glance at the circle of dead grass, before saying to Ann, "Vandalism? Oh, I hope not, dear. After all you've been through lately, it would be so unfair." Then she turned to the lieutenant and said, "But who would do such a thing? I suppose it must have been some of the local children?"

"Very likely," the lieutenant said. "But we have our eye on most of the troublemakers, so I wouldn't worry about it happening again out here. A word to the ringleader is usually enough to get them to lay off."

"Well, I certainly hope so," Mrs. Nichols said. "And I guess it might have been worse, the way so many children act today."

"A whole lot worse," the lieutenant agreed. "All the same, compared with some of the other kids in the country, we haven't got too bad a problem here in Walton."

After receiving several more of the lieutenant's reassuring observations, Mrs. Nichols said goodbye and returned to her house, while Lieutenant McGill put away his camera, zipped up his canvas bag and followed Carr and Ann back to the patio. When she offered him a drink he readily accepted, saying that a cool beer would go well on such a humid afternoon.

The three of them sat on the patio and the lieutenant took a swallow or two of beer, frowned, and folded his arms across his chest. "All right," he finally said, "I still don't like it any better than before, but I think there's enough to go ahead with. One thing is sure—your grass was killed by whatever was run through the sprinkler. Which leaves the real question—why was it done?"

"And you'll try," Carr said, "to find out whether Lloyd was poisoned or not?"

Lieutenant McGill nodded and looked at Ann. "If you'll give me the particulars—the town where your husband's buried and the name of the cemetery—I'll make some calls and get the thing started today."

Ann went inside, and when she returned with the information the lieutenant jotted down several names and telephone numbers in his notebook. Then he took another swallow of beer and said, "Tuborg—very nice, Mrs. Cunningham. Most people don't appreciate a good Danish beer. I guess your husband used to like it?"

"No," Ann said, "Lloyd rarely drank beer. Alex told me that once in a while he liked Tuborg, so I got some for him."

The lieutenant's eyes betrayed a brief spark of interest. He smiled and said, "I admire your taste in beer, Mr. Carr."

There was a long pause. The lieutenant sipped his beer again, and then he said, "Well, I'd better finish up here and get back to my office. I'm not really sure, though, what I hope the pathology boys will come up with. For my own sake, of course, their findings had better be positive. I don't run the police department, you know—and if the tests prove negative, I'll have the chief on my neck, wanting to know why in hell I requested an exhumation in the first place. As my old boss, Alvin Rosenberg, used to say, 'A policeman's lot is not a happy one.'"

The lieutenant looked at Carr and Ann. "On the other hand—if I were you—I'd be hoping the report shows no evidence of digoxin or anything else. I think things will be a whole lot easier for both of you, if it's completely negative."

"I don't follow your reasoning," Ann said.

The lieutenant swallowed the last of his beer and shook his head. "Mrs. Cunningham, I wonder if you really understand what you and Mr. Carr have set in motion? Suspicion of murder and an investigation means there's going to be talk—and lots of it. Your helpful neighbor, Mrs. Nichols, is probably on the phone right now, chatting happily with one of her many friends. 'Lloyd Cunningham hardly dead a week, my dear, and now the police have just been out at his house, taking pictures and poking around. They're *saying* it's vandalism, but obviously they're suspicious of something else.'"

The lieutenant got to his feet. "And when it starts getting around that I've asked for an exhumation order—and believe me, in a day or so someone will talk and the news will be all over town—then the local gossip factory will really start working overtime."

They walked around to the front of the house and the lieutenant slid behind the wheel of the dark coupe. "So what you think is," Carr said, "that Ann and I have opened some kind of Pandora's box, without realizing what's likely to pop out?"

"When someone starts talking about poison and murder," the lieutenant said, "all sorts of things usually start happening."

"But we had to come and tell you about it," Ann said. "Because we believe—*strongly* believe—that Lloyd was killed."

The lieutenant nodded. "I understand, Mrs. Cunningham. But do you and Mr. Carr understand? If the tests show that digoxin *was* used, people will start talking about how it was done and who did it—and when it's a question of a man being murdered, usually the first person the gossips start talking about is the man's wife. And, if there's one handy, about her youthful and charming boyfriend."

Carr and Ann stared at each other for several moments, and when Carr finally looked up again, he saw that the lieutenant was observing them closely.

Lieutenant McGill switched on the motor and put his car into gear. "You'll be hearing from me in a couple of days, Mrs. Cunningham. As soon as I have something to report."

Then the coupe made a turn in the street and headed back to police headquarters, and Carr and Lloyd Cunningham's widow went back into the house on Willow Brook Lane.

12

BY NOW IT WAS DUSK, the end of a long summer afternoon. Carr made drinks in the kitchen, and then he and Ann sat together on the living-room couch and watched through the picture window as a line of storm clouds swept in from the west. Soon it grew darker, and as they switched on the lamps, the first drops of rain began to patter against the glass.

"Your policeman got here just in time," she said. "By tomorrow, with the solvent washed away, we might never have convinced him."

"Sooner or later, I think he would have seen the light anyway," Carr told her. "The lawn would still be a mess. And don't forget Mrs. Nichols—she saw the ABC man and Mr. Englehardt."

After a pause, Ann said, "Maybe I did misjudge the lieutenant at first. Once he started describing his own troubles at headquarters, his foot-dragging began to make more sense."

"According to Arnold, McGill's an honest cop. So he'll do what has to be done about the tests. Then we'll find out how well he can handle a case of homicide."

The wind was rising and rain pelted against the window. A lightning flash brightened the room for an instant, followed by a roll of distant thunder. Carr poked at the ice cubes in his glass. "Once the news gets out, Ann, will you mind the gossip very much?"

"Well, nobody likes to be called a murderer, do

they?" She looked at him thoughtfully. "How will you feel about it?"

Carr shrugged. "Sticks and stones, as the saying goes. I guess I'll be able to look at it that way." He allowed himself a smile. "Still, if I'm going to be known around town as your official lover, I'd just as soon it wasn't an empty title."

She drew close and began to run her fingers lightly through his hair. "You are my lover, Alex. And I feel I'm yours—that I've belonged to you ever since I first knew you wanted me. Anything else doesn't matter, does it? It's only a technicality."

"A rather important one, though."

"Which we can take care of soon. Whenever you like."

"Tonight?"

"Why not, love? There's no reason for us to wait any longer."

When they'd finished their drinks he suggested they go out for dinner, but she said she'd rather stay at home, especially with the rain coming down so hard. There were steaks in the freezer and she could make a salad and, for a touch of extravagance, there was a Lafite '73 that the man in the wine shop had said was ready for drinking.

Despite all their efforts, though, the dinner was not a festive one. She looked unusually wan, and later, as they sat with their coffee in the living room, he was surprised to see the beginning of tears in her pale blue eyes.

"Whatever's the matter?" he said.

"Everything, Alex. Just a few hours ago, when you called up and said you were coming over, I felt so happy. I hadn't felt like that for ages."

"I felt pretty good myself."

"And I began to make plans. We were going to spend the whole afternoon somewhere, only the two of us, maybe have a picnic. With nothing on our minds, no worries or troubles. I wanted it to be our real start together—a beautiful start—and then everything went wrong.''

"I'm afraid it did," he said.

"Because you noticed the lawn. And after you did, because you went on thinking about it. And now we know the way Lloyd really died...and it's horrible."

He held her close and murmured that before long things wouldn't seem so bad, and after a time she grew calmer. She rarely smoked, but now she told him she needed a cigarette. After she'd lighted one he gave her his handkerchief and she touched at her eyes.

"You don't know how bad it was," she told him. "Before supper, out in the kitchen. When I turned on the tap to wash the lettuce. Last week, Lloyd had used the tap, too. He'd stood right by the sink where I was standing, and he'd filled his glass and gone outside...and the poison had killed him.''

"I know, darling.''

"And then, Alex, it really hit me. Mr. Englehardt, or whoever he is—why, *he'd* done the very same thing. Come inside—into my own kitchen—and turned on the tap and run the water there. But why only in the kitchen? How could he be certain Lloyd hadn't used one of the bathrooms? So just to be sure he probably went through the entire house and turned on all the other taps. And had a good look around, while he was doing it. Here in the living room, inside my bedroom...with Lloyd already lying there dead, outside in the sun....''

When she fell silent Carr held her even closer for a time. Finally he said, "We're going to lock up the place now, and then get out of here. We'll both feel a lot better over at the cottage tonight. You can follow me in your Buick—just put some things in a bag and we'll get started.''

She agreed without protest, and he returned to the kitchen with their coffee cups and started the dishwasher while she went inside and packed some of her clothes in an overnight case. They decided to keep on several small lights, made sure that the doors and windows were locked, and then walked to the garage and put her case in her car.

The rain had stopped, but the night air was still heavy with moisture. Carr drove slowly, keeping her Buick in the rearview mirror. A few minutes later they parked by the front of the cottage and he carried her case up the flagstone walk.

By the time they had switched on some of the lamps and settled themselves in the living room, she already seemed in better spirits. She took a swallow of brandy and the color began to return to her cheeks. "You were right," she said after a while. "I needed a change of scene."

"Feel more like yourself again?"

She nodded and looked around the room. Then she rose and walked over to the desk that stood by one of the front windows. "Is this where you do your work?"

"Sometimes. Mostly in the winter. But when the weather's warm, I like to sit out back."

"Typewriter put away. Papers neatly stacked. I see you're a tidy person."

"I'm not really. But every couple of months things get too sloppy, even for me. So I give way to virtue and straighten things up."

"I'm glad to hear it. I wouldn't like to think there wasn't *something* for me to try to improve."

He watched her stoop and look closely at the single

photograph on the desk. She picked it up by its silver frame. "Is this—was this Eve?"

"Yes. I took it on our honeymoon. We went to Bermuda. Not an especially original place to go."

"You didn't tell me she was so lovely."

"No—I don't suppose I did."

She returned to her chair and took another swallow of brandy. "Did you have all this furniture when you lived in New York?"

Carr shook his head. "No, after Eve died I decided to sell almost everything. I took the cottage furnished. I've added the desk, and a couple of extra chairs and some filing cabinets. The only thing I kept was that Chinese vase on the table. It was something she loved, so I brought it along."

"It's beautiful. I noticed it the moment I came in. Her taste must have been. . .remarkable."

He crossed the room and sat on the arm of her chair. "Will you do me a favor?" he said.

"If I can."

"Then please stop comparing yourself to my late wife. You're not on trial, you know. My God, darling—do you think I'm sitting here, running you through some kind of comparison test?"

"Well, I'll try. But it's hard for me not to feel some. . .concern."

"And what about me? Do you want me to start asking myself how attractive I am, compared with Lloyd?"

"That's different. You still loved your wife when she died—Lloyd and I were going to get a divorce."

Carr looked down at her and smiled. "Which still hasn't kept me from wondering whether he was much of a lover or not."

She returned his smile. "Anything I told you would make me sound bitchy," she said. "So I think I'll fall back on that old political cliché—no comment."

When they'd finished their cognacs Carr said he would show her the rest of the cottage if she liked. He carried her bag into the bedroom, opened one of the closets, and pushed aside some of his clothes. "There's lots of space, but move any of my stuff tonight if you need more room. Tomorrow we can fix things the way you like."

Crossing back through the living room, he led her to the spare bedroom and bath at the other end of the cottage. In the bedroom two chairs were piled high with books, and on the bed there was a clutter of still more books, newspapers and magazines.

She peered through the open doorway and wrinkled her nose. "I see what you mean about messy."

"Well, it's a sort of catchall, and sometimes it does get out of hand. Now the kitchen's over here—I keep that very tidy."

The pantry shelves and the contents of the refrigerator seemed to meet with her approval, and then they returned to the living room where she circled slowly, finally stopping a few feet from the French windows at the back. "I like it here," she finally said. "You were lucky to find it. Purley's Cottage is a real gem."

"An ideal bachelor pad. Arnold heard it was to let, so I came down, saw it and decided to stay."

She had been gazing at the floor, and now she took a step back and said, "God, I'm a fine one to talk about messy. Look at what I've already tracked inside."

Next to the French windows, on the edge of the carpeting, were several large deposits of mud. "Did you really do that?" he said. "I don't remember your standing by the windows."

"Now that you mention it, I don't remember, either."

"Then I must be the culprit," he said. "Only how

in the world did I get my shoes so muddy? When we left your place we stayed on the driveway—which is paved—and once we got here, we came up the flagstone walk. . . ."

He stooped and touched the carpeting. When he rose, he murmured, "It's still damp, though. Quite fresh."

After a moment's thought, he took off his shoes, examined them carefully under one of the lamps, then held them out to her. She looked at the soles and saw they were dry—and free of mud.

Before she could question him, he raised his fingers to his lips and winked broadly. Stooping over, he whispered in her ear, "Just play along with me. Don't ask why—I'll explain in a couple of minutes."

Straightening up again he said in an unnaturally hearty voice, "Well, will you look at that—I'm afraid I'm the culprit after all. My shoes are foul with mud. I must have got them that way when I went out to the shed, just before we came in."

"Yes, I can see it was you," she said.

"But it doesn't matter, I'll get everything off the carpet tomorrow. Time now for other concerns. For one thing, I'd better show you how the shower works. It's sort of tricky, and I wouldn't want you to scald yourself through sheer ignorance."

In dumbshow he beckoned her to follow, and then, talking some nonsense about how they would have to shop for food the next day, he led her into the bathroom.

"Once you know how the shower works, there's nothing to it," he said, and reaching out, gave the handle a full twist. The water gushed out with a roar, and he put his mouth close to her ear. "Speak very quietly," he said in an urgent voice. "And listen to me. Somebody was here tonight—inside the cottage—while I was over at your house."

"Because of the mud?"

"That's right. It must have been after the rain began. Maybe they dropped by, saw that I wasn't home and decided to pop in and plant a few bugs around—that seems to be their style—while they had the chance. In the living room. Maybe in the kitchen. Who knows where?"

"Christ," she whispered, "do you mean they can hear whatever we're saying?"

"That's my guess. Unless we block out the sound with something else, like running the shower. So from now on, until I can get McGill to come out here tomorrow and vet the place for bugs, no mention of Lloyd or Englehardt or anything to do with it. Will you remember?"

"Of course," she whispered. "We just talk naturally, avoid topic A, and pretend we don't know anyone's been here."

"That's it."

He started to turn the shower off, but she caught him by the arm. "Alex—how do you know they left?" Her grip grew tighter. "They could still be here, hiding somewhere."

"We'll have a look now," he told her.

He turned the shower off and pretended to laugh. "Got the idea, darling—first make sure the water's on *full*—then, when you know it's not too hot, there's no problem."

"I see," she said, and followed him back to the bedroom, where he hunted around among a pile of books and yellow legal pads until he found a flashlight.

"Before we go to bed, I'll show you where I keep things," he said. "Make our housekeeping easier tomorrow. I'll give you a complete Cook's tour of the premises.

He shoved the clothes around in the bedroom

closets, but no one was concealed there, and the substantial amounts of dust that had gathered under the
bed seemed undisturbed. Still talking about his
bachelor habits they returned to the living room. She
glanced at the empty fireplace, then walked over
and picked up the heavy brass poker.

She hefted it, swung it a couple of times in a short
arc to test its weight, and said, "Where do we go
next?"

"First, let's admire the furnishings in here. Then
I'll show you the kitchen and the spare bedroom."

They found nothing behind the draperies or the
couch. After that they examined the kitchen and the
spare bedroom and bath, but both areas seemed undisturbed.

"Is there any place else I ought to know about?"
she said. "Where does that door lead to?"

"The cellar."

"Shouldn't we have a look?"

"If you like. There's nothing much down there except the furnace and some wood for the fireplace—
but I suppose we might as well complete our
rounds."

She took a fresh grip on the poker and signaled that
she was ready. He opened the door, switched on the
light and cautiously led the way down a short flight
of shaky wooden steps.

A single naked light bulb left the small cellar
in shadows. He swung the flashlight around slowly.
The room was musty and cool—and appeared to be
empty.

"Not a whole lot of space down here," he said. He
took a deep breath and then stepped briskly around
to the back of the furnace.

But no hidden figure was crouching there, waiting
for them.

The only other possible place of concealment was

in a corner of the cellar, behind the pile of firewood.

"As you can see," he said, "when winter comes, we'll be well provided for. Let it snow, let it storm."

She came up behind him and raised the poker. They exchanged a glance, and he said, "We may as well have a look, don't you think?"

As if in reply, a sharp scraping sound echoed behind the woodpile.

"Oh, my God," she whispered, "there's somebody there."

They held their breath and the sound came again. And then without warning a couple of logs broke loose from the pile and crashed to the floor.

They stood frozen. Mesmerized.

Before the sound of the falling logs had died away there was a sudden movement, and the next moment, from the top of the woodpile, they saw two small angry eyes glaring at them.

"It's a rat!" she said. "Alex—I can't *bear* them!"

"No, I think it's only a squirrel," he told her. "They've been down here before."

There was a moment's silence and then a mass of gray fur leaped upward to the ledge of the cellar window, squeezed through an invisible opening, and was gone.

A few sweeps of the flashlight showed that the room was deserted now. He took her free hand—as cold with sweat as his own—and led her back upstairs to the living room where they opened the cognac and refilled their glasses.

After a while, when their nerves were steadier, they washed and put away the glasses, and then she told him she was tired and ready for sleep.

"But I wish you'd show me how the shower works again," she said, "It does make me nervous. I'm not at all sure I remember which way the handle turns."

Puzzled, he followed her to the bathroom and dutifully turned the shower on. Above the rush of water he whispered, "What's the trouble?"

The sudden bloom of color in her cheeks surprised him. "Alex...have you thought about tonight?" she whispered. "I mean, when we're in the bedroom. My God, those creeps might be able to hear every word we say."

He kissed her hair and nodded. "Yes, Ann, I've thought of that."

"But sweetheart...have you *really*? I mean, I say all sorts of things—people usually do...."

"I know. I'm not exactly a silent lover myself."

"And I do more than just *talk*—Christ, love, I'm quite sure that sometimes I become extremely, well, damn it all, I become extremely *audible*."

He kissed her again and said, "You want privacy, and that's what you'll have. Complete acoustical privacy, guaranteed to frustrate anyone at the other end of a bug."

While she took a shower he went around the cottage testing the doors to make sure they were locked. Then he took a shower, too, and afterward, returning to the living room, unplugged the radio and carried it into the bedroom.

"Music to soothe us before we sleep," he said. "I think you'll like it. We get very good reception here."

"What sort of music?"

"Classical. Terribly elevating—in the spiritual sense, of course."

He got into bed and switched on the set. "It's an all-night station and the announcer has a very mellow voice. I wonder what he's got on now?"

The station was playing a symphony. "Beethoven," she said.

"Yes, the *Pastoral*. I think we're in luck. After all, it might have been Scriabin, or *The Pines of Rome*."

He turned the volume higher, and saw her smile at last. "Everything all right now, darling?"

"Yes, everything's perfect," she said.

He held her close in the dark for several moments, and then all at once she whispered, "Alex, darling," and made him stop.

"Something the matter?"

"No, everything's fine. I was only thinking—tonight...it's just possible...I might be very, *very* audible. So please, angel, play the radio a little louder."

"A good thing we don't have any close neighbors," he murmured, and with a twist of the dial, flooded the cottage bedroom with the sound of music.

13

THE NEXT MORNING, directly after breakfast, Carr called the police. He told Lieutenant McGill he believed someone had entered Purley's cottage the previous evening, and that considering prior events it was all too likely the intruder had bugged the premises before departing. The lieutenant did not sound especially cordial. He complained of having a busy morning ahead, but promised to come out and inspect the cottage as soon as he could, maybe in an hour or two.

While Ann was dressing, Carr put away the dishes, then walked outside and carried several chairs to the far end of the lawn. Satisfied that any conversation about Lloyd Cunningham or Englehardt would be safe from eavesdropping he settled himself on one of the reclining chairs and stretched his legs out comfortably in the sun.

Ann soon joined him on the lawn. She was wearing a loose-fitting man's shirt and a pair of paint-stained jeans, and she'd brought along her sketch pad and a couple of pencils.

"Going to do a study of Purley's Cottage?" he said.

"No, I thought I might do you," she told him. "Would you mind sitting for your portrait?"

"I'd be flattered. I can't remember the last time someone wanted to use me as a subject."

"I'd rather you took off your glasses, though. And could you sit up a little bit straighter—that would make it easier for me."

"Glad to oblige. But are you *really* going to work today, Ann?"

"I work every day—don't you?"

He pushed himself up higher on the chair and slipped his glasses into his shirt pocket. "No, I only work in stretches," he said. "Sometimes I write for two or three months without a break. After that I stop, and take some time out to think."

"And what are you thinking about today?"

"Oh, just a few personal items. Like how happy I feel this morning. And how much I love you."

"That's nice. And what else?"

"Well, since you asked, I've been thinking, too, about a rather interesting problem. Specifically, if we're right about what happened to Lloyd, whether you or I might also be in danger of getting ourselves killed."

She continued to sketch with unhurried pencil strokes. "And what did you decide?"

Carr didn't reply at once. Instead he stared across the lawn at the huge sycamore and at the grinning leprechaun that stood beneath it. Then he said, "It's hard to tell for certain. Too many of the facts are still obscure."

"Maybe, but one fact seems plain enough to me," she said. "Someone wanted Lloyd dead because of what he'd learned about them. And I was his wife, and you were working with him. So, *if* they think we know as much as he did, then I don't see why they wouldn't go ahead and try to kill us, too."

"Of course, you may be right," he said. "Unless it wasn't what Lloyd *knew* that got him murdered, but what he was threatening to do with the information."

"Meaning blackmail?"

"Would you say he was capable of it?"

She laid the pad down on her lap and considered the question. At last she said, "Lloyd always was thinking about money. Big money. And more than ever lately. Yes, it's possible he could have turned to blackmail."

"Your marriage must have been very difficult at times," Carr said. "Especially after you found out what he really was like. In fact, since there weren't any children involved, I'm surprised you stuck it out as long as you did."

She took up the pad and began to sketch again. "I wanted our marriage to work. I was quite desperate to see that it did. Because my first one hadn't been much of a success, either."

"I didn't know you'd been married before."

"For a year. When I was nineteen. Does it make any difference?"

"None whatever," he said. "As soon as our current problems are disposed of, I'm going to ask you to marry me . . . no matter how many previous husbands you may or may not have had."

Before long they heard a vehicle braking by the front of the cottage, and then there was the sound of a car door being slammed. "That must be the lieutenant," Ann said. "He got here sooner than he thought."

Carr looked at his watch and nodded. "Which means I'd better get up and show him around." Even as he climbed to his feet, though, he realized they were mistaken—it wasn't the lieutenant coming around the side of the cottage, it was his sister, Joyce.

She waved a greeting and then joined them on the lawn. As she lowered herself into one of the vacant chairs, Carr watched her steal a glance at Ann, and was amused to see how quickly she sized up their new domestic arrangements. It took only an instant—her eyes went wide, she smiled to herself—and then the altered circumstances had been catalogued and accepted.

Carr returned to the reclining chair while his sister, with an air of agitation that was unusual for her, apologized for arriving unannounced. "I try never to drop in without telephoning you first," she said, "because I don't like to interrupt your work. But when I was passing the cottage just now, I decided—on the spur of the moment—that I needed to have a talk."

"Something been upsetting you?" he said.

"Well, yes—one or two things have. In fact, to tell you the truth, dear, I'm really not at *all* myself today. Everything's gone wrong from the moment I got up this morning. Starting with Arnold telling me—out of a clear sky—that we can't leave on our vacation next week the way we'd planned."

"That doesn't sound like Arnold," Carr said.

"No, it doesn't, but that's what he told me. A case that's very important to the firm and that no one but the big chief can handle properly. So he has to stay and try to get things straightened out, and if that means he can't get away until the fall or the winter, then he simply can't."

"No wonder you're upset," Carr said. "What will you do—go up to Maine by yourself?"

"Of course not. What fun would I have alone? Or even with Jennifer—did I tell you, by the way, that she got back from her tennis camp this week, and we were thinking of taking her along? But I *won't* take her anywhere, not without Arnold. Alex, you remember what it was like—did you ever take a vacation without Eve?"

"No, we always went together."

Joyce swung around and appealed to Ann. "Or did you and Lloyd...oh, dear, I am upset this morning. That was tactless of me, wasn't it?"

Ann smiled and said, "No, not at all. Although, as a matter of fact, Lloyd and I had been going our separate ways for a while—ever since we decided that our marriage was just about over."

"Over?" Joyce said blankly.

"We'd pretty much agreed it was a while ago. So naturally, after that, I no longer cared a whole lot what he did with his spare time."

Joyce took a cigarette out of her handbag and lighted it. Then she turned and said to Carr, "Well, I don't know *why* you got me off on the subject of vacations—Maine isn't what I wanted to talk to you about—it's something much more important. Really, Alex, I'm at my wit's end. I simply don't know what to do about Jenny, and for that matter, neither does Arnold—though of course you mustn't tell him I said so."

"What seems to be the trouble? Has my favorite teenager selected the wrong boyfriend?"

"I almost wish she had," Joyce said. "No, it's worse. Tennis. She did very well at her camp. Too well. And now she says she has no intention of going to college. She insists she wants to turn professional as soon as possible, she doesn't even see the point of finishing high school. She and Arnold are at each other's throats—and I'm an old fogy, too, so nothing I say makes any difference, either. You must help us, Alex, and I'm sure you can. You're the only intelligent person I know that she might listen to."

"All right, I'll have a go at it," he said. "When would be a good time?"

"Come and have dinner with us tomorrow night. We'll go over to the club. Either you can talk to her then, or you can arrange to get together with her some other time. I'll leave the details to you. It doesn't have to be right away, but you must try to talk some sense into her."

Joyce rose to go. As she picked up her handbag, she said to Ann, "And please—tomorrow—come with

Alex. I'd like you to meet Jenny, and it will be so much more relaxed if you both come.''

After Joyce had left, Carr stretched out in the sun again and Ann resumed her sketching. ''I could see that your sister was very upset about Jenny,'' she said. ''But all the same, to *me*—today, right here and now—listening to her did seem odd.''

''In what way?''

''Her troubles sounded so normal. So conventional. And meanwhile, here the two of us are, wondering about Lloyd, and sitting and waiting for the police to arrive. It's as though somehow we'd made some kind of dreadful mistake and wandered into a totally different world. . . and a very ugly one at that.''

''Apparently that's what we've managed to do,'' he said, and then pointed across the lawn. ''Mr. Purley over there—that's what I call the grinning little devil—is a leprechaun. Do you know very much about leprechauns?''

''Only that they're found in Ireland, and are said to have certain magical powers.''

''They're also said to be crazy about gold. They hide it in caves, I believe, or bury it in the ground. Lloyd was a bit too tall to have been one himself, but all the same, I think he had some of the same ideas as the little people. And whenever you have dealings with a leprechaun, you're likely to find yourself in trouble. . . and in a world that's neither normal or conventional.''

''Because of the gold?''

Carr nodded. ''I think, at least in our case, that might be part of the answer.''

They idled away the rest of the morning, fixed themselves lunch, and while they were cleaning up afterward, Lieutenant McGill arrived in an unmarked coupe. He dropped the now familiar blue canvas travel bag in the living room and then Carr and Ann took him on a brief tour of the shed and the cottage. Finally they showed him the deposits of mud on the carpet near the French windows.

The lieutenant knelt on the floor to examine the mud. "Looks like someone might have been out in the rain," he said. "The stuff's still a little damp, Mr. Carr. Are you sure you didn't track it in yourself last night?"

"We didn't come in that way," Carr told him. "We used the front door."

"I see."

"In fact we didn't go near this part of the room—not until Ann happened to notice the mud."

"You were here last night, Mrs. Cunningham?"

"Yes. . . I was," Ann said.

The lieutenant stepped outside and began to study the French windows. "You've got a few scratches here on the wood," he told them. "They're freshly made, too. And the lock's not much—pretty easy to jimmy it open, if you wanted to get inside."

"Is that what you think somebody did?" Ann said.

"It certainly looks that way. Probably used a pocket knife or a small screwdriver. Clumsy, though. Not what you'd call the work of a professional burglar."

"Maybe the man was in a hurry," Carr suggested.

"That could be. Have you had a chance to check your valuables, Mr. Carr? Anything missing, as far as you know?"

Carr laughed, and then shook his head. "No, nothing seems to have been taken, Lieutenant. People don't usually steal manuscripts, and I don't have much else they'd want. Except maybe the hi-fi, and that Chinese vase over on the table."

The lieutenant cleared his throat and coughed into his hand. "Would you mind bringing me a glass of water?" he said. "It's time I took some more vitamin

C. Helen says if you don't take the stuff every couple of hours, it won't do you any good, so I'd better stick to the routine."

Ann brought him a glass of water and he swallowed two pills. He coughed again, swore to himself, and then said with a scowl, "Okay, sick or not, I'll take a look around."

He picked up the canvas bag and drew out a pair of black cotton gloves and a few small manila envelopes. "How many phones in the place?" he said to Carr as he pulled on the gloves.

"Just two. One's over there on my desk. The other's back in the bedroom."

They watched as the lieutenant went to work. He sat at the desk, eyed the telephone thoughtfully for a moment, and then, leaning forward, began to run his gloved fingers slowly along the underside of the kneehole.

"Somewhere near the phone," he explained, "is the first place to look. Hello—what have we got down here?"

He pushed the desk chair back, stooped over, and peered into the kneehole. A moment later he was standing up, a small metal object cradled in his hand.

"You've found one?" Ann said.

"As big as life. And if I remember right, it looks like the same foreign model we found before in Mr. Carr's Volkswagen."

The lieutenant edged the device into a manila envelope and placed the envelope inside his canvas bag. Then alternately squatting, crawling, and standing on various pieces of furniture, he examined the rest of the living room. The painstaking search, though, produced nothing else.

Next the lieutenant led the way into the bedroom, where he peered around until he spied the telephone on the bedside table. Sitting on the bed, he ran his fingers along the underside of the table. Before long he straightened up, a second metal object in his gloved hand.

"More of the same," he said.

Carr and Ann followed him, as he went through the rest of the cottage, but the lieutenant discovered nothing more. When he'd finished, he put the gloves back in his bag and prepared to leave.

"I'm pretty sure your place is clean now," he said to Carr. "Later on today, when I get a chance, I'll make out a report on what I found here—forced entry by way of the French windows, and the two bugs."

Then he turned and said to Ann, "And as soon as I get the pathologist's report, Mrs. Cunningham, you'll be hearing from me about your husband."

After the lieutenant had left, they spent the rest of the afternoon doing chores—Ann returned to the house on Willow Brook Lane to pick up her mail, another suitcase of clothes and some additional painting gear, while Carr typed a few pages of notes for his Egyptian article, and then took the Volkswagen into Walton to shop for food and wine.

Well before dusk they drove north toward Bridgeville, parked near Silver Lake, and spent the early evening eating a picnic supper on a gently sloping hill above the water. By nine o'clock they were back at the cottage, and by ten they were fast asleep.

SOMETIME DURING THE DARKEST PART of the night Carr awoke, stirred by an uneasy feeling that something was wrong. He reached out tentatively, found only tumbled bed linen, and remembered with a rush of pain another empty bed two years before, when Eve had gone away to the hospital. . . .

He opened his eyes and looked around the room. At first he thought he was alone, but then he saw a tiny red glow at the foot of the bed. Ann was sitting there, cross-legged like an Indian, smoking a cigarette.

"Been awake long?" he said.

"A while, I guess." She put the cigarette out and returned to bed, pulling the sheet over her shoulders and then winding her arms tightly around him.

"What were you thinking about?" he said.

She reached up and touched his cheek. "I wanted to tell you out at the lake, but I knew you didn't want to talk. So—I just let it go."

"Better tell me now."

She touched his cheek again. "Alex, I'm a direct person, that's the way I'm made...but I think you aren't exactly like me—maybe sometimes, to spare yourself, or someone else, you'd rather avoid talking."

"Maybe so. What have I been avoiding?"

"This morning, when I said I'd been married before, you didn't ask me about it."

"Why should I? It happened a long time ago."

"But I *need* to tell you."

"Well, if you must, love, then go ahead."

"His name was Tom. Tom Rubin. We were both going to art school. He was several years older than I was, and really gifted. We had an affair, but it wasn't working out, and then, just when I was going to tell him I meant to break it off, his draft notice came. I hated the war, and I was still very young and I guess pretty mixed up about a lot of personal things—I desperately wanted to leave home and have a place of my own—and I felt sure if he went to Vietnam, he was going to be killed. I mean, I really believed it. So I married him, and he didn't have to go into the army, and after we'd lived together for a year—a damn miserable year, too—we got a divorce."

"Is that it?"

"Yes."

"Nothing more?"

"No."

"Well, okay, so now I know about your first marriage. Anything else I've been avoiding?"

"Just one other thing, darling. I *know* it's what a man usually does—but really, I'm not half as fragile as you think, so I do wish you'd stop trying to protect me from the truth."

He raised her hand and slowly kissed the tips of her fingers. "The truth about what, Ann?"

"The danger we're in."

"What makes you think I've been hiding the truth?"

"Because I remember—and I'm sure *you* remember—what the lieutenant told you a couple of days ago. After you found the first bugs in your car and took them to his office. He said you were in danger then—and that was even before anyone suspected that Lloyd might have been killed."

Carr leaned against the pillow and closed his eyes. After thinking for a while he said, "All right, maybe I have been holding back. We are in danger—of course we are. But it took somebody quite a while to decide that Lloyd was in the way, and I'm hoping they aren't in any particular hurry to finish us off, either."

"And in the meantime, we just sit patiently and wait . . . and do absolutely nothing?"

"Darling, I haven't tried to do anything yet, because I'm counting on the police to bring in the killers very quickly—long before Mr. Englehardt or the ABC man decide to draw a bead on us."

"And if you're wrong about the police?"

"If I'm wrong about them, love—if the police *don't* seem to be doing the job very briskly, then of course we aren't just going to sit and wait. We'll say to hell with the authorities, and try to get everything settled on our own."

His words seemed to satisfy her. She said little else, curled up against him even more snugly, and soon fell asleep. And after a long time, Carr fell asleep too.

IT WAS WELL AFTER SUNRISE, and the telephone on the bedside table had begun to ring. A woman's voice said, "Mr. Carr?"

"Yes."

"This is Helen McGill. If you can, John would like you and Mrs. Cunningham to meet him this morning at eleven o'clock."

"We'll be in his office then," Carr said.

"No, please come to our house. John called in sick this morning. He's staying home and wants to talk with you here."

"Fine, Helen. I'm sorry to hear the lieutenant is under the weather, but in any case, we'll be over at your place in a couple of hours."

"And there's one thing more John asked me to tell you. He said the report came in early this morning. It *was* digoxin—a very large dose."

"I see," Carr said. He put down the receiver and told Ann what he had just heard, and then after a subdued breakfast they drove into Walton, to learn what the ailing lieutenant would have to say about homicide.

14

THEY FOUND the McGills' two-story frame house in one of the older sections of Walton, a few quiet blocks away from the center of town. Helen McGill, heavyset and voluble, greeted them at the door and for a minute or two she talked about books and the public library and what a great success the recent fair had been. Then she told them her husband was waiting to see them on the back porch.

"I suppose he feels miserable today," Ann said as they started down the hall.

"Not half as miserable as I do," Helen told them cheerfully. "It's a case of Jekyll and Hyde—most of the time John's as good as gold, but whenever he gets sick, he starts acting like a bear with a sore nose."

The lieutenant was seated at one end of an old-fashioned screened porch, dressed in bedroom slippers, summer pajamas and a faded blue bathrobe. A formidable barricade of health aids surrounded him—a card table with two pitchers of fruit juice and a pitcher of water stood on one side of his chair; a smaller table with a box of Kleenex and a clutter of medicine bottles, glasses and spoons stood on the other; and at his feet there was a large waste basket, already half-filled with discarded tissues. When Ann and Carr appeared the lieutenant didn't bother to rise, but instead motioned them to a pair of cane chairs that had been placed a dozen feet away from where he was sitting.

"Don't get too close," he cautioned them in a fretful voice. "I could still be in the infectious stage...or so that imbecile of a doctor told me this morning. It's your lousy vitamin C, Helen—I don't know why the hell it didn't work this time. And will you please bring me some more orange juice—I've got to do a lot of talking now, and my throat's burning up before I start."

Ann murmured something sympathetic and then Carr said, "Your wife told us about the report coming in—about the digoxin anyway."

The lieutenant regarded them glumly, with watery, red-rimmed eyes. "That's what they found all right...and plenty of it. Probably introduced into the ABC tank in soluble form as tincture of digoxin, or maybe digitoxin. The pathologist said it would have been tasteless either way and wouldn't have caused nausea in someone already habituated to considerable quantities of any digitalis derivative. So there's no doubt about it, Mrs. Cunningham. Your husband was killed deliberately, by someone who was very anxious to have him dead."

"And now," Ann said, "you're going to find out who that somebody was."

The lieutenant poured himself out what appeared to be a glass of grapefruit juice, and with a series of grimaces, swallowed it down. Then he drew a tissue from the Kleenex box and blew his nose.

"Of course I'm going to do my best to find out who murdered your husband," he said. "That's my job. Only there's one thing you and Mr. Carr should understand. As I told you before, I don't run the department on my own. I've got a boss, and sometimes he likes to look over my shoulder. As a matter of fact, he's very interested in Lloyd Cunningham's death. First real homicide we've had here in Walton in the two years since Edgar Timmins got himself elected chief-of-police.''

The lieutenant looked at them cautiously. ''Either of you happen to know Ed personally?''

When Ann and Carr told him no, the lieutenant glanced at his watch and said, ''Well, that little oversight will be taken care of today. The chief should be here any time now. Early this morning, as soon as the report came in, he wanted to haul you both down to headquarters, but I said no—I'm still running the investigation—so we'll all get together here, and at a civilized hour.''

''I suppose,'' Carr said, ''he wants to see if we have any other information, besides what we've already told you.''

''That might be what's on Ed's mind,'' McGill said. ''Or maybe he just wants to size you up for himself.''

The lieutenant cocked his head and looked at Ann. ''I believe, Mrs. Cunningham, you've lived in Walton longer than Mr. Carr—are you at all familiar with Ed Timmins's career?''

Ann thought about the question briefly before she said, ''If I remember correctly, he used to be one of our town selectmen. He served for several years. Then last fall he won a seat in the state legislature down in Trenton.''

''That's right,'' the lieutenant said. ''Ed Timmins is a politician—not a real cop at all. I remember once, back in the city, Alvin Rosenberg said to me, 'McGill, the policeman who wants to stick around and collect his pension should avoid two things—any junkie pointing a gun, and any politician with dreams of glory. And believe me, McGill, of the two, the pol is a lot more dangerous.' ''

Before anything more could be said the doorbell rang, and they heard Helen McGill ushering someone into the house. There were footsteps, and then a tall broad-shouldered man in sports slacks and an open-neck shirt came out on the porch. He nodded to the lieutenant, asked how he was coming along, and then bowed to Ann and shook hands with Carr. He put his attaché case on the card table, sat down on a vacant chair and with a dazzling smile that featured two rows of perfect white teeth, assured both Ann and Carr he was indeed glad to meet them.

What principally surprised Carr was the chief's age—he could hardly have been more than thirty-five—which meant that he was at least fifteen or twenty years younger than the veteran police officer who served under him. And he was a remarkably handsome man—perhaps "photogenic" would have been the more accurate term. Now he took an empty pipe out of his pants pocket, and sticking it into his mouth, favored Carr with another smile.

"I'm sure that by now," he said, "John has told you about the pathologist's report...." The smile disappeared as he turned to Ann, and he said with an air of grave sobriety, "The fact that your husband *was* murdered, Mrs. Cunningham, though you'd already suspected as much—the confirmation of it this morning, must have come as a shock to you, and I'm grieved—the entire department is grieved, of course—to learn for a certainty that your suspicions were justified. All the same—" and he turned back to Carr, "—at least we know where we are now, and what must be done. It goes without saying that we have both of you to thank for alerting us to the real situation, and for getting us started in the right direction."

Edgar Timmins paused and thoughtfully tapped his front teeth with the stem of his pipe. "We're grateful, of course, for the information you gave us. And we're impressed, Mr. Carr, by the way you

worked things out. It was very clever of you. Ingenious—nothing short of ingenious.''

The words were friendly enough, the praise apparently sincere, and yet Carr felt an immediate stir of
irritation and mistrust. From long practice in inter-
viewing strangers he had developed a useful sixth
sense, a kind of professional radar system, that often
in the past had alerted him to hidden obstacles and
dangers—to the ostensibly candid man or woman
who was saying one thing, while secretly thinking
something quite different. And now the radar was
on, and the warning signals growing stronger.

"It's kind of you to say so," Carr replied, "but
once I'd spotted the solvent on the lawn, the rest
followed logically enough. In any case, the important
thing is that we *did* guess right about Lloyd's death—
that he didn't die of natural causes—so that you and
the lieutenant can track down the people who murdered him.''

"And that most certainly is what we intend to do,''
Chief Timmins said. "In fact, Mr. Carr, from the very
beginning we've been working along those lines.
We've assumed that we might be faced with a homicide case, so I've had John here and the rest of the
department check into every aspect of the account
you gave us. Though I must say that so far we
haven't come up with a very clear idea of who killed
Mr. Cunningham. . .or even of why he was killed.''

"I should have thought the reason for Lloyd's
death was perfectly obvious," Carr said. "He'd discovered the Amazon Factor. . .and that the A. and S.
Chemical Company was criminally responsible for it.
So they killed him before he could go public with
what he'd learned.''

"That *is* one possible explanation," Timmins said.
"But I must confess that it strikes me as less than fully persuasive. Many companies have been caught do-

Ing irresponsible or illegal things before this, but how often have they murdered anyone to conceal their crimes?"

Ann leaned forward and said, with a slight edge to her voice, "And what do you think might be a better explanation?"

Chief Timmins favored her with another dazzling smile. "I find it a little difficult to say this, Mrs. Cunningham, and believe me, it's far from being the department's official position yet—I think each of us still has a very open mind—but any police force in the world will tell you, when someone is murdered, the question of motive must be fully explored. And in nine cases out of ten, the motive proves to be anger, greed or sexual passion, while the perpetrator of the crime almost inevitably turns out to be someone well-known to the victim."

Carr saw Ann's face slowly turn red. She said very quietly, "I simply do *not* believe it. I simply cannot believe my own ears."

Carr leaned over quickly and took her hand. "A little patience, darling. Let the chief go on. You did ask him for another explanation, so let's hear the rest of what he has to say."

Edgar Timmins bit on his pipe for a moment, and then said in a reflective voice, "Here, I think, is what an unbiased observer might conclude about Lloyd Cunningham's death. He had a wife—a most attractive wife—who no longer was in love with him. She and another man were having an affair, and they wanted to marry, but unhappily, Cunningham was not cooperative."

"I'm afraid that simply isn't true," Ann said. "Lloyd and I already were thinking about a divorce a number of weeks ago. And it was as much my husband's idea as mine."

"But did you file for one? Were any papers drawn up?"

"No—we hadn't got to that stage yet."

"I see. Well, since there really is no evidence to indicate otherwise, the unbiased observer might very well conclude, as I've already said, that Cunningham had been difficult—he would agree to a divorce only as the injured party—and alimony, or a substantial property settlement, was out of the question.

"Now at this point," Timmins said, "wishing to keep an eye on his wife's lover, Cunningham approached the other man with a business proposition. He told him that he'd discovered something called the Amazon Factor, and that together they could expose the A. and S. Chemical Company and make a tidy sum doing it.

"Naturally enough, the lover and Cunningham's wife discussed the matter, and before long they worked out a scheme—a very ingenious scheme—that would solve all their problems. They would kill Cunningham, making it look as though he had died of natural causes. Then, they would 'discover' that such was not the case, and inform the police that Lloyd Cunningham actually had been murdered—not by themselves, of course, but by the mysterious and elusive 'Mr. Englehardt,' and by the equally mysterious and elusive 'ABC man.'

"The police would thank them for the tip, and would try, without success, to track down Mr. Englehardt and his colleague. The police would also attempt to establish a demonstrable connection between Egon Ritter and the murder, but again, they would fail. The case would remain unsolved. Eventually, after sufficient time had passed, the wife and her friend would be free to get married without undue suspicion—and now, being in possession of

Lloyd Cunningham's entire estate, could settle down to a life of comfortable domestic bliss."

Carr grinned and said quickly—before Ann could break in—"It's complicated, all right—and it's ingenious—but I do think your theory has a few interesting holes in it."

Timmins grinned good-naturedly in turn. "Well, I didn't say it was completely watertight, Mr. Carr. Not yet, at least. What do you see as some of the holes?"

"For one thing, you say that Cunningham was killed by his wife and her lover—but if they did murder him, then who were Englehardt and the ABC man? Because remember, Mrs. Nichols saw them."

"Yes, she certainly saw them both," Timmins said. "We know that a 'Mr. Englehardt' was there, and we're going to make every possible effort to find him. I would say he was someone the murderers hired for the day—probably some out-of-work actor one of them had known, back in New York. Most likely they fed him a cock-and-bull story about playing a harmless practical joke on a nosy, busybody neighbor—some sort of yarn like that—and then paid him enough so he'd be willing to act the part of an E.P.A. official for an hour or two."

"And the ABC man? Another out-of-work actor they hired?"

"I doubt it, Mr. Carr. Another actor would have escalated the risk too much."

"Then who *was* the ABC man?" Ann said. "Why not Cunningham's wife, rigged out in a fright-wig? Or maybe her lover, who also was up in New York the entire afternoon?"

"Ah, but was he *really*?" Chief Timmins said. "He told the police he was there, but did anyone who knew him actually see him in New York, after he had lunch with his agent? Because otherwise, there's no denying the fact that he had plenty of time to leave the tanks on Willow Brook Lane in the morning, catch the 10:55 A.M. to New York, eat lunch there, and then take the early train back instead of the four o'clock—and by midafternoon appear once more on Willow Brook Lane as the ABC man. By the way, Mr. Carr—your opinion on that point would be very useful—do you think Mrs. Cunningham's friend met anyone after lunch, who could provide him with an alibi?''

Carr took off his glasses, rubbed his eyes, and thought hard for a while. Finally he shook his head. ''No, I'm sure he didn't meet anyone he knew in the city, or coming home afterward.''

''Any *other* holes, Mr. Carr?''

''Just one or two. The first being the question of who turned on the sprinkler and removed the incriminating water glass, since it couldn't have been the hired actor?''

''Quite right. It was the ABC man—Mrs. Cunningham's friend—who took care of those details.''

''I see. Well, it might have been done that way. Which leaves us with the problem of Egon Ritter. And it *is* a problem. Because one word from him, and your whole theory is blown sky-high.''

''I'm afraid, though,'' Timmins said, ''there isn't likely to be any such word from our friend Ritter.'' He looked over at Lieutenant McGill. ''Yesterday, John, down at the plant, he wasn't very forthcoming, was he?''

The lieutenant shook his head. ''No. Ritter didn't have a whole lot to say. He *did* admit Cunningham had been to see him a couple of times, but said it was only to discuss a plan to improve hospital benefits for some of the plant workers. He had no idea what the Amazon Factor was. He also said he'd never telephoned Mr. Cunningham at his home for any reason—and as far as you were concerned, Mr Carr, he'd never even heard of you."

"But that's a damn lie," Ann said. "I know Lloyd and Ritter were on the phone—I heard them myself— and they certainly were talking about Alex."

The lieutenant poured some water into a glass, and then began to swallow it in small delicate sips. "That may be true, Mrs. Cunningham—I'm not saying it isn't—but if you look at it from the police point of view—it's strictly your word against his."

"All right, then," Carr said, "what about the bugs? And the break-in at Purley's Cottage—the scratches on the French windows and the mud that was tracked inside. *Somebody* did all that, didn't they?"

"Why not the lover himself?" Timmins said. "Think about it—what could have been easier for him than to plant a bug in his own car, a couple more in the cottage, then add a few scratches and a little mud—and presto, Englehardt or Ritter or somebody else from A. and S. not only is involved in an elaborate effort to spy on an innocent man, but at the same time automatically becomes the prime suspect in Cunningham's murder."

Ann slowly shook her head. "Jesus H. Christ—an *unbiased* observer? That really is a laugh, isn't it?"

"No, love—the point holds up," Carr said. "I'm afraid the chief is right. There's nothing to prevent a man from bugging his own house or his own car. The only question is, why did he put two different bugs in the Volkswagen—wasn't that being a little redundant?"

"But he didn't put in *both* of them," Timmins said. "When he placed his own bug under the dashboard, he had no idea another bug already was in the car."

"And who put the first one in?"

"Why, Cunningham, of course, in order to get the goods on his wife and her lover."

Carr leaned back in his chair and laughed softly. "My God, you have got it all figured out, haven't you? Except for one point of logic, which I'm afraid leaves such a large hole in your theory, Chief, that even you might not be able to patch it over. Our criminals—the wife and her lover—have killed Lloyd Cunningham, as they'd planned to do from the start. His death has been attributed to natural causes, and Lloyd is safely dead and buried. Nothing now stands in the way of their getting married and settling down to the marital bliss you mentioned before.

"But no—for some incomprehensible reason—they cannot let well enough alone. Instead, they go to the police and say, 'Lloyd Cunningham did *not* die of natural causes. He was murdered, and you must prove it, and then catch his murderers. In the name of all that's reasonable, why did they do that? Why did they stir up needless suspicion and run needless risks when they'd just succeeded in committing a perfect crime?"

"But the crime they'd committed," Timmins said, "was far from perfect, and they knew it. So the risks they ran were not needless—they *had* to be taken."

"And why was that?" Carr said.

"Lloyd Cunningham carried two policies on his life, each written by a different insurance company and each taken out a number of years ago, when doubtless his heart was much sounder. Very substantial policies, Mr. Carr. According to his attorney, Arnold Daniels, who drew up Mr. Cunningham's will, each policy would pay his widow the sum of three quarters of a million dollars. Now, as we all know very well, insurance companies are inclined to drag their feet a bit, whenever they're asked to pay off a very large claim. More often that not, they will look for a suitable excuse to avoid making any payment at all—preferably an escape clause that will void the entire policy. And in this case, both policies contain such a clause. In the event that Lloyd Cunningham committed suicide, his widow would forfeit her claim to the sum total of a million and a half dollars.

"So you see," Timmins said, "Mrs. Cunningham and her friend had a difficult problem to resolve. They could kill Lloyd Cunningham with a massive dose of digoxin and make it seem that he'd died of natural causes, but when they went to claim his insurance, as they would have to do to settle his estate, either company, merely as a routine business procedure, would make every effort to obtain an exhumation order and a pathologist's report—and if that happened, the fat would be in the fire. Because the report would lead the company and the civil authorities to one or the other of two distressing conclusions: either that Mr. Cunningham had killed himself with an overdose of digoxin, and his widow was not entitled to a penny of his insurance; or else that Mr. Cunningham had been murdered, leaving Mrs. Cunningham and her friend as the logical—indeed, as the only—plausible suspects.

"So I think you'll agree, Mr. Carr, that the murderers ultimately found the best possible solution to the problem. They decided that Mr. Englehardt and the ABC man *had* to appear at the house and be seen by Mrs. Nichols—and afterward the police *had* to be informed of it, and persuaded to believe that Cunningham had been killed by two strangers, as a consequence of his involvement with the A. and S. Chemical Company and something called the Amazon Factor. Once this had been accomplished, Mrs. Cunningham and her friend would be left in the clear, and eventually they would be in the enviable position of collecting two very nice checks, totaling a million and a half dollars, as a reward for all the work they'd done, and for any uneasy moments they might have experienced while committing their crime.''

There was a long period of silence. Finally Carr said, "It's really very neat—if you could just prove that Mrs. Cunningham's friend really had been the ABC man, I imagine that would about wind things up.''

"Or else Mr. Englehardt," Timmins said as he stuck his pipe away in his pants pocket and got to his feet. "I think his testimony would be even more of a clincher. And we *will* find him, Mr. Carr. Sooner or later, I assure you, the police will find him and put him on the witness stand.''

"Before you do that," Ann said, "I should think you'd want to take another look at your theory. Because it certainly leaves out one very important item.''

"And what is that?''

"The tapes Lloyd made. Wouldn't it be better to listen to them first before deciding who killed my husband?''

Chief Timmins picked up his attaché case and nodded. "Mrs. Cunningham, that's just what we hope to do. As I said in the beginning, the department has a completely open mind about your husband's death. All I've been trying to accomplish here today is to outline one possible explanation for it. Naturally we're as anxious to hear the tapes as you are. No doubt, for security's sake, he put them away in his safe-deposit box at the bank, planning as he did, to hand them over to Mr. Carr later on. So, I'm going to obtain a court order this afternoon and notify the tax people and on Monday you and your attorney, along with someone from the department, will open the box, and then we'll be able to hear everything that Mr. Cunningham's invaluable tapes can tell us about what he'd learned.''

Chief Timmins favored Ann and Carr with a last dazzling smile, assured the lieutenant he knew his way out, and then disappeared in the direction of the front door. When it was certain he'd gone, Carr said, "I think we'd better be getting along, too, Lieutenant. Only before we go, I'd like to ask you a question."

"Anything you want, Mr. Carr."

"Do you agree with Timmins? Do you really believe that Ann and I killed Lloyd Cunningham?"

Before the lieutenant could reply, the kitchen door swung open and Helen McGill came in, carrying a frothy pitcher of orange juice. She put it down on the card table and said, "Of course he doesn't think anything of the kind. What a ridiculous idea, isn't it, John? These two couldn't possibly have murdered Lloyd Cunningham, not in a million years."

"Helen, will you please keep your nose out of this," the lieutenant said. "It's police business—*official* police business—it isn't any concern of yours. My God, no wonder it took you so long to get me a little fresh orange juice—if you hadn't been so busy listening to what was being said in here, and had been fixing the juice the way you were supposed to. . . ."

Helen McGill lowered herself into a chair. "Why don't you just drink some of it," she said, "and you'll feel better. And after that, you can answer Alex's question."

The lieutenant drank a glassful of juice and said glumly, "All right, Helen, get off my back. Can't you see how sick I am today? I need sympathy, not your infernal hectoring. No, I don't buy the chief's scenario, Mr. Carr. There's plenty of circumstantial evidence against the pair of you, but I'm still not buying it."

"Well, obviously Chief Timmins is convinced," Ann said. "So why not you?"

"I'm not running for anything, am I, Mrs. Cunningham? Do I want to be a senator one day soon, and go off to Washington? Or move with Helen down to Princeton, and live in the governor's mansion?"

"No other reason?" Carr said.

"Sure—an even better one. I'm a cop, and Ed Timmins isn't. I know what killers are like, and he doesn't—most of the time I know, anyway. So let's just say it's my ability to analyze character a little. Neither one of you strikes me as the type to commit murder. Not greedy enough. Not self-absorbed or vicious enough. And to tell you the truth, Mrs. Cunningham, I think in the case of Mr. Carr, not smart enough, either."

"But John," Mrs. McGill said, "Alex is a writer, so how can you possibly say—"

"*Will* you keep out of this, Helen? By not smart enough, I only mean he doesn't have the right kind of smarts—it's different from book intelligence . . . do you know what I'm saying, Mr. Carr?"

"Yes, I believe I do," Carr said.

Then he and Ann stood up, and while they were saying goodbye, she asked the lieutenant if she would see him on Monday, when her husband's safe-deposit box was opened.

"If I don't die of pneumonia first," he said. "Or if Timmins doesn't decide to go himself. And Mrs. Cunningham, I gave your friend here some advice one time—I told him to forget about protecting his sources and to look for a good place to hide. Well, I've got another piece of advice for him now . . . and for you. Get out your beads, or your prayer rug, or your Bible, or whatever they recommend in the religion of your choice, and begin to pray. Just pray that Lloyd Cunningham made the tapes the way he said, and that he found out plenty of juicy stuff about Ritter and the A. and S. Chemical Company. Because with someone like the chief so eager for headlines, you'll need all the help your late husband's tapes can give you."

The lieutenant turned away and began to uncap one of his medicine bottles, and Ann and Carr walked through the house and out to the quiet street where the summer sun was reaching its zenith. As they climbed into the Volkswagen, Carr said, "I don't know about you, darling, but I don't usually put much stock in beads and prayer rugs. I lean more toward the old adage—the Lord helps him who helps himself."

"Meaning you've finally lost some of your faith in the local constabulary?"

"All right, Ann—don't rub it in—so I made a mistake about the police. Well, now it's time to rectify it. I hate to do their job for them, but finding out who murdered Lloyd seems like the best way to keep us out of the pen."

"And where do we start?"

"At the beginning, love—with Ritter and the chemical company. I'll give him a call, and try to see him this afternoon."

"Even though, as our friend the chief pointed out, most companies don't go around killing people merely to conceal their crimes?"

"Perhaps A. and S. is a little different. Lloyd certainly thought so—"

"Yes, and look where it got him."

"We'll be more careful. Lloyd went in with his guard down."

Carr switched on the motor and eased the Volkswagen out into traffic. "And while I'm having my visit with Ritter," he said, "you might go back to the house and have a run through Lloyd's personal papers."

"What do you want me to look for?"

"Anything that connects him with Ritter. Or that shows what he'd found out about the Amazon Factor, and the setup at A. and S. By the way—I don't suppose Lloyd kept a gun around the place?"

"No, he never had one. Alex, why do you ask?"

"I thought that someday soon—just possibly—a gun might come in handy."

Ann lighted a cigarette and dropped the match into the ashtray. "Jesus," she said, "you certainly know how to soothe a woman's nerves."

Carr grinned and said, "I wouldn't want you to think your hero has feet of clay, darling—but the truth is, my nerves aren't exactly in perfect shape, either."

15

WHEN THEY'D FINISHED LUNCH at the cottage, Ann said she would drive her own car back to the house on Willow Brook Lane and spend the rest of the day searching through Lloyd's papers. She told Carr she'd be dressed by six-thirty for their dinner at the club with Joyce and Arnold, and then suddenly she held him close and made him promise to be careful, especially if he went to see Egon Ritter that afternoon.

After she'd gone, Carr sat at his desk and telephoned the A. and S. Chemical plant. He was prepared for a cool reception and was not surprised to hear Ritter's secretary say that the plant manager was not in his office. No, she didn't know *when* he might return—perhaps not for the entire afternoon—could she be of any help? Carr explained that he was a journalist engaged in writing an article on the fertilizer industry, and that he wanted to make an appointment with Egon Ritter to discuss the company's operations.

There was a pause, and then Carr heard the faint sound of a hand being pressed over the telephone speaker, while the secretary talked with someone nearby. After a few moments the hand was removed and the secretary said, "Mr. Carr, I *think* I see Mr. Ritter down the hall. Yes—he'll be with you in a minute—he's just coming into the office."

After a decent interval to maintain the charade,

Ritter came to the phone. Carr repeated his story and Ritter said, "I'm afraid I cannot make any new appointments just now, Mr. Carr. My schedule is very crowded. Possibly, though, by the end of the month—"

"Today would be better," Carr said. "Lloyd Cunningham, a friend of mine, suggested I get in touch with you."

For a moment Ritter hesitated. When he spoke again his voice seemed to be pitched a trifle higher, and Carr thought he could detect for the first time the slight trace of a foreign accent. "Oh, yes—*Lloyd Cunningham*, from the hospital—I remember speaking to him. Health insurance, I think. Mr. Carr, my secretary tells me that one of my appointments has been unexpectedly canceled today, so perhaps I can see you after all. Do you have any transportation to get out to the plant?"

"I'll drive over," Carr said.

"Then I'll tell the gateman to expect you. Should we say about four o'clock?"

"That will be fine," Carr told him. He hung up, glanced at his watch, and began to consider what his next move should be. Clearly a look into the setup at A. and S. was long overdue. After a few minutes' thought, he got out his address book, telephoned the *Times* in New York, and asked for Harley Spenser, an old friend and a veteran reporter who specialized in financial news.

When the social preliminaries had been disposed of, Carr explained the object of his call. "A. and S. Chemical?" Harley said. "Well, offhand it doesn't ring much of a bell. Lots of small privately owned companies around. What did you say they specialize in?"

"Fertilizers," Carr told him. "And fungicides."

"Okay, I'll try and get a rundown on them when I can. How fast do you need it?"

"As soon as possible."

Harley's laugh was tolerant. "A matter of life and death?"

"I believe *two* lives are involved. And one of them happens to be mine."

"You serious, Alex?"

"Completely."

It was several moments before Harley spoke again. Then he said, "All right, in that case maybe I can speed things up—I'm starting to get a few vibrations. I think a while ago there *was* an article published that might have mentioned A. and S. Let me ask some people around here, and then I'll get back to you."

A half hour later Carr was sitting behind the cottage, sipping a Coke and eyeing the grinning Mr. Purley, when the telephone rang. "Alex, I've got a lead for you—a friend of mine at the *Journal*, Gus Phillips, did a piece on the chemical industry a couple of years ago. And there's one paragraph where he mentions A. and S. It's just what you told me—relatively small, privately owned, a leader in the fungicide market. . . ."

"Is there anything else?" Carr said.

"No, that's about all. But look, let me give Gus a ring now and see if I can catch him in. He probably found out more than he was able to use in his article, and if so maybe he'd take a quick look through his files. I'll get back to you as soon as I've talked with him."

At two-thirty Harley called again. "I've just set it up for you with Gus," he told Carr. "I said you were a good friend of mine and needed anything he had on A. and S. So he's looking through his notes, and if you call him, say in a quarter of an hour, you can see what he knows."

Carr thanked Spenser and, when enough time had passed, telephoned New York again. Gus Phillips was expecting him. "I've gone over my notes on A. and S.," he said, "and I can give you some of the picture. Remember, though, I didn't do the company in depth—they were almost peripheral to the main thrust of my story—and besides, as I'm sure you know, being a privately owned corporation means they don't come under the S.E.C.'s disclosure regulations. So, if they want to, they can keep a lot of what they're doing under wraps."

"I understand," Carr said.

"All right, from what I could learn, A. and S. is twenty-five years old, small to medium in size, incorporated in Delaware. The company manufactures agricultural products, including a fungicide that is the recognized leader in its field. It's said that a good deal of U.S. grain benefits from its use—supposedly our annual wheat crop alone is twenty or thirty percent higher than it might otherwise be, if another, less effective fungicide were used."

"Quite a valuable product," Carr said. "Where do they manufacture it?"

"They started with three plants—one in Colorado, near Denver, another in Missouri, and a third one in Maryland. Then, about seven or eight years ago, the company developed a greatly improved version of the fungicide, so they acquired a new plant in New Jersey—in Walton, in fact—to begin producing it."

"How about the company's earnings?" Carr said. "Were you able to get a line on them?"

"Sure, they gave me the figures—after all, they knew I could always go to somebody else, like an ex-employee, and get a lot of the same dope."

"Did the figures suggest anything?"

"Not very much—except I did notice the profits a few years back looked kind of skimpy. When I questioned them on it, I got the usual corporate gobbledygook—high start-up costs, unprofitable products written off—nothing you really could say was out of line. So I queried them on the obvious—if the fungicide part of the business provided them with such a narrow profit margin, why had they decided to pour more money into another plant?''

''And what did they say?''

''More gobbledygook—lower start-up costs this time; larger productive capacity leading to a higher cash flow—theoretically it was all possible.''

Carr thought a moment and then said, ''Look, when it comes to corporate finance I'm a mere babe in the woods. So let me ask you a dumb question—could A. and S. be a conduit for another group or organization, an illegal or a criminal one—even the Mafia? Could they use a company like A. and S. to launder money they were getting from other sources?''

''I don't see why not,'' Gus said. ''Here and there around the country you probably could find a few setups like that. Funny you should bring up the Mafia, though...someone else asked me about the criminal brotherhood only a few weeks ago.''

''Really? That sounds interesting.''

''Well, it wasn't very interesting for me. I was here in the office one afternoon, when this fellow Cunningham came roaring in, saying he wanted to know all about A. and S. Chemical. Told me he'd read my article, and figured I was an expert. His line was that A. and S. had been underpaying their taxes down in New Jersey, or some such nonsense, and he was going to protect the public interest by lowering the boom on a bunch of crooks and grafters. The man was a real pain in the ass. I thought I'd never get rid of him.''

''Did he ask for any particular information?''

''No, nothing special. Except the address of the company's offices here in New York—he didn't know it—and the names of the company officers.''

"You don't happen to have the names handy?"

"Sure...they're right here. Let's see—Chairman and C.E.O., Archibald Dempsey. President, Darrell Baker."

"Do you have any biographical material on them?" Carr said.

"No, but it should be easy to find. Just try the basic reference book—it's called *Who's Who in Finance and Industry*. They're sure to be in it."

"I don't suppose you ever met Dempsey or Baker yourself?"

"As a matter of fact I never did—when I dropped by their offices they were both out of town, so I queried the young fellow who seemed to be in charge—I think his name was Smith—and he gave me most of the stuff I wanted. Later on he answered the rest of my questions on the phone, and as you know, I had no reason to call on A. and S. again."

After Carr had thanked Gus Phillips for his help, he locked up the cottage and drove to the Walton public library. He sat at a table in the rear and went carefully through the latest edition of *Who's Who in Finance and Industry*. There was no listing for either Archibald Dempsey or Darrell Baker. Evidently the senior officers of the company had no interest in routine publicity or self-promotion. Personal privacy—if not total anonymity—seemed more in their line.

IT WAS APPROACHING FOUR O'CLOCK when Carr began to drive through the spacious grounds of the A. and S. Chemical Company. On every side were neat lawns and carefully tended trees and shrubs, and then, at a considerable distance from the gates, there appeared a succession of one- and two-story industrial buildings that housed the plant itself. Arriving at the parking lot behind the administration building, Carr gave his name to the gateman, who directed him to a parking space next to the manager's. The contrast between their two cars was striking—his own modest untidy-looking red Volkswagen parked alongside Ritter's gleaming black Mercedes 450SL.

A few steps brought Carr to the reception desk, where he was asked to wait. There was a brief delay and then he was told that the assistant manager, Mrs. Ritter, was on her way down.

"Did you say *Mrs.* Ritter?" Carr asked the receptionist.

The young woman nodded. "Yes—people are always surprised at first, because married couples don't usually work together like that. But after you've been here at A. and S. a few days you get used to the idea."

Carr scarcely had digested this curious morsel of information, when the elevator door swung open and Mrs. Ritter appeared. She was blond, rather noticeably broad in the hips and shoulders, but still extremely good-looking. And her eyes were memorable—green and bold, perhaps even wanton—but above all steady and unflinching. Eyes that immediately announced a person with determination and purpose—a woman who would have to be reckoned with.

She led the way to the elevator and then down a long corridor to the manager's office. Inside, a paunchy heavyset man already had got to his feet. Egon Ritter put out a soft hand, smiled for a moment, and motioned Carr to take a seat.

When Mrs. Ritter had disappeared into the adjacent office, Ritter tilted back in his chair and said, "Mr. Carr, there's no point in wasting your time or mine, so I suggest we get down to business. When we spoke before, you mentioned Lloyd Cunningham. I've heard of his unexpected death, of course—a real tragedy—but what interests me is the connection between Mr. Cunningham and your wish to visit me today?''

"The connection is quite simple," Carr said. "I'm interested in learning more about Cunningham's death. You not only knew him, Mr. Ritter, but at the time when he died, you and Cunningham were working closely together."

"Me and Cunningham? Working together? But that is completely ridiculous."

"It is?"

"Why, I hardly knew the man. I'd met him only once or twice here in my office. We talked about health insurance."

"I'm afraid you talked about a good deal more. One night Mrs. Cunningham overheard you and her husband on the phone. From what was said, it was plain that you and Cunningham were collaborating on some sort of scheme, and that you'd been doing so for a considerable length of time."

"She told you that?"

"She did."

"Then I'm afraid," Ritter said, spreading his hands and smiling broadly, "that poor Mrs. Cunningham is in error. People do make mistakes, you know."

"Lloyd Cunningham certainly did," Carr said, returning Ritter's smile. "Quite a lot of them in fact. And one was such a big mistake that it finally got him murdered."

Ritter's manner underwent a change. His good humor seemed to ooze away, replaced by a sharp-eyed wariness. He blinked several times, not unlike a lizard trying to decide whether or not to shift its position in the sun, and then he said very deliberately, "I'm not quite sure I heard you correctly."

"I said that Cunningham made a mistake, and that somebody murdered him."

Slowly Ritter's ruddy cheeks began to pale. "But

I'm sure our local newspaper said he'd died of a heart attack?''

"Don't newspapers make mistakes, too? The police have been here to question you. Would they have done that if Cunningham had died of natural causes?''

"I was puzzled when they came snooping around, yes. It did seem strange, but I never thought—I simply never imagined—that anyone might have killed him.''

"And since they did, Mr. Ritter, is there really any reason to suppose that one day they might not want to kill his partner, as well?''

Ritter no longer could conceal his distress. He touched his fingers to his forehead, which gleamed with tiny beads of sweat. "Mr. Carr—I don't understand—why have you been telling me all this?''

"Because I want to know what you and Cunningham were doing before he died. I think that with your help, I may be able to figure out who killed him.''

"And then take your information to the police? So that before very long, the whole world will know why Lloyd Cunningham was murdered.''

"Can you think of any reason why I *shouldn't* go to the police?''

"No. . . of course not." Ritter drew out a handkerchief and wiped his forehead, and Carr saw the dark patch of sweat under his arm. "Mr. Carr. . . I'm not very well just now. I've had a bad virus the last couple of days. I'm afraid I must leave you for a few minutes. . . ." He opened the connecting door to the next office and said, "Maria, I'm going to the washroom for a little while. My virus is back again. Please come in and keep Mr. Carr company while I'm gone.''

Ritter already had left the office by the time his

wife entered and took her husband's place behind the desk. If she shared her husband's anxiety, she concealed it perfectly. Her manner was calm and, like her smile, was apparently meant to be friendly.

"Your news has upset Egon very much," she said. Leaning forward, she reached for the intercom on the desk with her forefinger, and flipped the switch lightly up and down. "This was open—my husband keeps nothing from me—I heard everything that was discussed."

"The idea of murder," Carr said, "usually upsets people."

"My husband has been on edge for a number of months. Ever since Cunningham first appeared. Threatening him—his livelihood, his career—but Egon, I'm sure, will tell you all that himself when he comes back."

"It should be very interesting," Carr said.

Maria Ritter stared at the closed office door through which her husband had left, then switched off the intercom. After a moment's hesitation, she fixed Carr with her steady gaze. "What I'm going to say, Mr. Carr, will puzzle you . . . but don't ask for an explanation. It would take too long. Just believe what I tell you, because it's important."

Carr nodded and said, "I'm listening."

"Be careful, Mr. Carr. During the next few days take no unnecessary risks."

"Why do you say that?"

"I told you—no explanations. Just remember what I say—exercise extreme caution . . . even with my husband."

Maria Ritter's expression was warm and earnest, but the meaning of its appeal was unfathomable to Carr. "Even with your husband, Mrs. Ritter? That's an odd thing to say, isn't it?"

"Odd . . . but true. If he should suggest your

meeting him somewhere later, don't go. Or if he should offer you a tour of the plant . . . make up some excuse for not accepting it. Do you follow what I'm saying?"

"I do," Carr said. "But not why you're saying it."

"Caution, that's all that matters. It might mean your life, Mr. Carr."

Someone was standing outside the frosted-glass office door. The handle turned and Egon Ritter came in. He apologized to Carr and thanked his wife, who stood up promptly and without another word returned to her own office.

When they were alone again Ritter settled himself behind his desk. "I'm all right now," he said. "A brief upset, but it's past. So let's return to business. You want to hear about Cunningham—very well, I'll tell you what I know, and I certainly hope that somehow it will help you."

Egon Ritter folded his hands and leaned forward on his desk. "Lloyd Cunningham first approached me a couple of months ago. He'd learned about the accident here at the plant last year and about the fact that apparently a part of the local population had been affected in a curious way by what he called the Amazon Factor. And he'd learned that not only was I in charge of the plant, but also that I had been the engineer responsible for some of its special design features—so that if the story of the accident came out, I stood an excellent chance of losing both my job with A. and S. and my professional reputation."

"Meaning," Carr said, "that Cunningham began with a touch of blackmail."

"Yes—in exchange for his silence, I had to cooperate . . . or else."

"And what did he ask you to do?"

"To provide him with as much information as possible about the company. Especially about the people who ran it, and the others whom he called the *real* owners. He said that if I helped him to get the goods on these criminals and malefactors of great wealth—that's what he called them sometimes—then he would give me a ten percent cut of whatever he received for his silence. At the same time, he said he'd make sure I would keep my job, which was what I wanted, far more than the money."

"And were you able to give him the help he wanted?" Carr said.

Ritter shook his head. "Not really—I'm afraid I was rather a disappointment to Cunningham. You see, though I've been with the company almost eight years, I've rarely had any contact with our top officials, and none at all with the other owners. I don't even know who they might be—I'm not paid to know such things, I'm only paid to run the plant. So all I could do was provide Cunningham with the limited information I had and later on, when he asked me, I was able to put him directly in touch with our president, Mr. Baker. Setting up their negotiations and sometimes acting as a go-between really was my major service to Cunningham."

"All the same," Carr said, "he must have learned something important about the company—something more than the fact that there had been an accidental spill here at Walton. Otherwise, the people at A. and S. wouldn't have been so eager to buy his silence. Tell me, Mr. Ritter, what do you imagine it was that Cunningham learned?"

"I have no idea," Ritter said with a frown. "He always told me as little as possible—after all, he was the general and I was the corporal. And he was a very secretive man—I suppose it's all down on the tapes he was making—but he certainly never told me what else he knew."

"And the owners of A. and S.—do you think Cunningham learned who they were?"

Ritter shook his head again. "I can't say for sure— but I think not. I believe when he died he was still doing a lot of guessing. And some of his ideas made no sense to me. He was like an old-fashioned text-book—unscrupulous robber barons with a defective product...bribing senators and congressmen... Watergate...illegal payments...Teapot Dome... sometimes the Mafia—all that sort of thing. And of course mixed up with everything else, so that you could never really tell the truth from the lies, was Cunningham's own greed—his wish to end up with a great deal of money."

The plant manager fell silent. Carr glanced at his watch and decided there was no point in prolonging the interview. He rose to leave, Ritter stood up, too, and then walked with him down the corridor to the elevator. While they were waiting, Carr said, "You've got an interesting operation here—one day I'd like to look over your plant."

"Of course," Ritter replied without noticeable en-thusiasm. "Perhaps in a few weeks you might give me a call. And in the meantime, let me know if I can help with your investigation. Poor Cunningham—it makes me sick just thinking about it."

CARR RETURNED TO THE PARKING LOT, drove back to the gates of the plant, and then took the narrow twisting country road that led to Purley's Cottage. As he sped through the early twilight he tried to sort out all that he'd learned—and failed to learn—from Rit-ter and his wife. It was clear that several essential pieces of the puzzle were still missing. Even so, it was possible to draw a number of inferences about the company Cunningham had been investigating and the people who ran it, as well as the circum-stances surrounding Cunningham's discovery of the Amazon Factor and his subsequent death. At any rate, one thing was certain—Lieutenant McGill had been squarely on target when he'd talked about smelling a fish, even if you couldn't see who was hiding it.

Gradually Carr's thoughts drifted back to the present as the Volkswagen reached the crest of a long steep hill. A few yards ahead, a heavy trailer truck already had begun its swift descent toward the valley. The Volkswagen picked up speed as it, too, started down the hill. Within moments the free-wheeling truck was only a couple of dozen yards ahead, thundering and swaying, and Carr decided to ease back to a safer distance.

When he pressed down on the brake, though, nothing happened. There was no resistance. He pressed the pedal again, this time as hard as he could. His foot drove heavily against the floor. He reached for the emergency hand brake and tried it. There was no response.

The brakes were dead. And he was hurtling down the hill directly behind the truck at sixty miles an hour.

His first thought was to swing left, accelerate quickly, and pass the truck on the way down. Once in the lead, he could reach the bottom of the hill safely, and then the force of gravity would take over and eventually bring the car to a halt. As he began to swing wide, a glance at the road ahead told him the plan wouldn't work. A succession of cars—at least three—were coming up the hill. Any attempt to pass the truck would lead to a head-on, hundred-mile-an-hour collision.

By shifting the clutch from fourth to third gear, he managed to reduce his speed, though only slightly. He tried to improve things further by shifting down to second, but found that he couldn't. Luckily the truck was still descending at full throttle. Moving a little faster than the Volkswagen now, it roared down the hill, and for several moments the distance between the two vehicles grew wider.

But it was only a temporary reprieve. Near the bottom of the hill was an intersection; as the truck approached it the driver would have to apply his brakes. The Volkswagen, unchecked, would career forward and smash full speed into the back of the truck—unless Carr could swing around to the right and run along the shoulder of the road, taking his chances with whatever obstacles stood in the way.

As they approached the bottom of the hill he pumped futilely on the brake and cursed Egon Ritter. The fat son of a bitch had set him up beautifully. First by having the attendant direct him to a space in the company parking lot next to Ritter's own car. And then by excusing himself for that trip to the men's room—a trip Ritter had never made. Instead he must have gone outside, loosened the emergency brake cable, and then, after cutting the Volkswagen's flexible neophrene brake line, wrapped some tape around the cut. The first time heavy pressure was applied against the brake the tape would rupture, the brake fluid would spill out and the Volkswagen would cannonade into something... with an excellent chance that the driver would be seriously injured or killed. A nice piece of ad hoc engineering. The fat, miserable son of a bitch.

They were down the hill now, the truck and the Volkswagen, racing in tandem toward the intersection. The ground was level and the truck began to lose speed as the brakeless Volkswagen rushed toward it. Carr turned the wheel slowly, and edged over to the shoulder of the road. At the last possible moment he swung right, around the truck, and onto the grassy shoulder.

The wheel twisted in his hands as he struggled for control. The shoulder sloped off into a ditch several feet wide and he steered the bucking Volkswagen into it. The ground was too rough; the Volkswagen banged into a rock—and then another. A tree loomed ahead. He turned the wheel, but not in time. There was a heavy jolt, the car lurched, then bounced along the bottom of the ditch. Another tree stood in the way. He couldn't avoid it. There was a second, final jolt, and his head struck the roof of the car as they began to turn over. . . .

At first he could only see things dimly. His glasses were dangling from one ear. Stunned by the impact, he tried to catch his breath and clear his head. Then he smelled gasoline.

The motor would still be hot—he had no more than a few seconds to get out of the car.

The Volkswagen was lying on its side. He tried to push against the door, but couldn't move his shoulders. The safety belt. He searched for it, tugged at it, finally found the release. He shoved at the door again. It was stuck. He pushed at it frantically with his hands, rammed it with his shoulder.

It sprang open and he hoisted himself up through the narrow opening, then rolled onto the grass. As he crawled away from the car on hands and knees he heard a roar behind him and felt a sudden wave of heat. He crawled farther along the ditch, turned around, and watched the Volkswagen burn.

16

SEVERAL MOTORISTS HAD STOPPED near the scene of the accident, and one of them had gone to a nearby house to summon assistance. First to arrive was an ambulance from the Emergency and Rescue Service; the driver stopped, and a young woman doctor climbed down from the cab to examine Carr and determine the extent of his injuries. It was soon agreed that he'd probably suffered nothing worse than the painful bruise on the left side of his forehead and the small but bloody cut from flying glass on his right cheek. When she'd finished applying a rather large bandage to the cut, Carr signed a release, and the doctor returned to the ambulance and sped away.

At almost the same time a new, red pumper truck, its siren screaming, arrived on the scene with an eager contingent of the Walton volunteers. By now the Volkswagen was little more than a smoldering skeleton, but the volunteers hosed it down anyway, sending up a spectacular cloud of steam in the process.

As the volunteers were preparing to depart, the borough police, represented by Officer Bowers, arrived in a blue squad car. Carr handed over his license, and the youthful policeman immediately recognized his name. "Oh, yes, Alexander Carr. I've heard about you and Mrs.—"

"Cunningham?"

Officer Bowers grew pink with embarrassment, at the thought of his professional lapse. "Yes—Chief Timmins had all of us out the last couple of days, asking questions along Willow Brook Lane. Now I guess I'd better go and get my book, and write down what happened here today."

Carr gave the officer an account of the accident, and then accepted an offer to be driven home in the squad car. Back at the cottage he telephoned Ann and said he wouldn't be able to pick her up before dinner after all—he'd had a little trouble with the Volkswagen—so instead, why didn't she come around to the cottage for him in the Buick?

She arrived a short while later, knowing that something had gone wrong, but unprepared for the sight that greeted her—the blood-soaked bandage and the long purple bruise on his forehead. At first she remained completely calm. She stared at the bloody gauze, then touched his forehead gingerly with her fingertips. "Jesus, darling," she said, "what did you do—get into a barroom brawl with Ritter?"

"No, it was all quite civilized," Carr told her. "At least it was until he tried to kill me by sabotaging the brakes. No harm done, though—just a couple of sore spots here and there."

"Is that really true, Alex?"

"I promise you—I've already been examined by a doctor and given a clean bill of health."

At which point she burst into tears and threw her arms around him, swearing tempestuously at Ritter for being a filthy swine, at Carr for rashly disregarding his own safety, and then at herself for being the cause of his injuries, his narrow escape from death, and all the trouble they were in.

Carr poured out two brandies and made her swallow one, and then they went to the bathroom, where she put a fresh bandage on his cheek. After that she bathed her eyes and reapplied her makeup, while Carr retired to the bedroom where he changed to a summer suit and selected a defiantly gaudy tie to wear to dinner.

As they drove toward the club he asked her if she'd had any luck with Lloyd's papers, but she shook her head and told him no. "I went through everything in the house—letters, bills, the desk in his study, his files in the basement. I even shook out the books in the library, in case he'd hidden something there. But if he ever wrote down anything about the Amazon Factor, or Ritter and the company, I simply couldn't find it."

"To tell you the truth," Carr said, "I didn't expect you would. Lloyd was too careful—and it really doesn't matter—we'll still get whatever we need from the tapes."

Had Carr and Ann wished to draw attention to themselves, their entrance into the large well-filled club dining room would have been a notable success. At least a dozen heads turned, and there was a moment of almost complete stillness, before talk resumed and the noise rose to its normal level again.

"The scarlet woman and her lover," Ann murmured as they began to make their way toward the Daniels's table.

"Either that, or my unusual war wounds," Carr replied. "I'm afraid I do look rather spectacular tonight."

Arnold Daniels stood up to greet them, one slightly elevated eyebrow the only sign of his astonishment. Joyce and Jennifer were less adept at deception, though. Joyce bit her lip, tried to appear airily unconcerned, and could scarcely wait till they were seated before she said, "Alex—dear God—are you all right?"

"I'm fine," Carr said, and turning, put an arm

around Jenny's shoulders and kissed her sunburned cheek.

"Well, you don't *look* fine," Jenny said. "You look awful, Uncle Alex. Just perfectly awful."

"I had an unusual golf match this afternoon," Carr replied. "Fellow lost on the 18th, blew his cool, and attacked me with a five iron. Proving, I'm afraid, that some people do *not* know how to lose very graciously."

"Aren't you going to tell us what really happened?" Jenny said.

"Maybe later on," Carr told her. "But at the moment, all we should be thinking about is food and drink."

Nobody mentioned his appearance after that, or asked for an explanation. Instead, they divided into two parties and, over a round of drinks, talked of more conventional things. Arnold and Joyce began to discuss the world of museums and galleries with Ann, and then encouraged her to describe some of her experiences as an art student in New York, while at the same time Carr was allowed to monopolize his niece. Jenny told him about her summer tennis camp, who the instructors had been, and the things she'd learned from each of them, before she and Carr switched to a discussion of the tennis world's current stars.

A second round of drinks arrived, then cold soup and finally the main course, and as the minutes slipped by Carr found it increasingly difficult to focus his attention exclusively on his niece. He and Jenny were talking about some of the old-time tennis greats—Bill Tilden and Helen Wills, Don Budge and Alice Marble—but part of his mind kept slipping away to more pressing concerns. To Police Chief Timmins, to the A. and S. Chemical Company, to Lloyd Cunningham and the Amazon Factor.

Now and again, too, he overheard snatches of the other conversation across the table—Ann was telling Arnold and Joyce about the rundown apartment she'd lived in as a student.

"There were three things I hated about the place," Carr heard her say. "The cockroaches all over the kitchen, the plumbing that always kept backing up, and the family of mice that holed up in the closet and wouldn't leave."

"Not *mice*," Joyce said. "I don't see how you endured it—I know that *I* never could have, Ann."

"And that's because," Arnold said, "you're a sybarite, sweetheart, exactly like me. You and I couldn't exist without the good things of life—which makes us Philistines—while on the other hand, being an artist, Ann has the moral courage to endure not only bad plumbing, but also small vermin."

Jenny had been planning on leaving early to join some of her friends, and as the coffee and dessert arrived Carr saw her glance at her watch. "How about coming over to the cottage sometime," he said, "and we can continue our tennis discussion?"

Jenny looked up at him with her large dark eyes—her one feature that never failed to remind him that she was Arnold's daughter. "And please the folks?" she said.

"And please me. Why not tomorrow, if you're free?"

"Sure, that's okay."

"Say at twelve o'clock? I'll give you a proper lunch—lean hamburger, cottage cheese, and all the salad and fruit you can eat."

Jenny told her parents that she had to go, said a polite good-night to Ann, and prepared to leave. Carr held back her chair and she stood up and kissed him on the cheek—the unbandaged one. "See you tomorrow," she said, and then, knowing she couldn't be overheard, she added, "I like your new girl friend, Uncle Alex. I think she's really neat."

With Jenny gone they all drew together for the first time. Joyce said anxiously, "You are going to see her?"

Carr said, "She's coming for lunch tomorrow, if you'll drop her off. The cottage at high noon. She and Uncle Alex will discuss things then."

Arnold took a swallow of coffee and smiled wanly. "Our hostage to fortune—my God, I wonder sometimes why people bother to have kids. Which doesn't mean we aren't grateful, Alex, for anything you can do." He looked at Carr and the smile faded. "But we aren't the only ones who've got troubles, are we? Obviously you've been leading an interesting life the last few days. Joyce and I would like to hear the details—unless you're too worn out and want to go home early?"

"No," Carr said, "tonight would be fine. Ann and I have plenty to tell you. Things got pretty hairy today with the local authorities—there's really a lot of ground we ought to cover."

Arnold glanced around the room and said, "It's still pretty crowded here. Why don't we go back to our place and have a talk?"

It was a drive of several miles to the Daniels's house, and since Arnold set off ahead of them at his usual high speed, it didn't take Carr and Ann long to lose sight of his taillights. As they followed along at their own slower pace, Ann told him that she'd enjoyed their dinner—she liked Joyce and Arnold—and Jenny *was* something special.

"Arnold's very upset, though," Carr said. "He doesn't fancy his only daughter becoming a tennis pro."

"She'll get over the idea before long," Ann said. "She's too imaginative and smart to want that kind of life. Jenny may be as pretty as her mother, but I'd be willing to bet she's got a lot of her father's brains.''

''She thinks you're sort of neat yourself,'' Carr said. ''Gave her stamp of approval before she left.''

Ann looked at him and said, ''You still look awfully pale, darling. You worry me—I hope you're really all right.''

''I wouldn't tell anyone but you,'' he said, ''but I hope so, too. Because I can't seem to make my brain work any more. Back there at dinner, I heard you say something to Joyce and Arnold that I thought might be important, and I was just about to figure out why, when Jenny interrupted—she said something about Alice Marble's second serve—and the whole damn thing went flying out of my head.''

''You'll work it out. Once you've had a good night's rest.''

''Maybe so,'' Carr said. ''Unless I'm over the hill before my time.'' Then he slowed down and turned off the main road into a large private driveway.

The Daniels's air-conditioned house was spacious and comfortable. Joyce and Arnold met them at the front door and led them through the carpeted hallway, past the formal dining room, and then down a short flight of stairs to the book-lined study. A well-stocked bar was there to provide drinks, and while Arnold took orders and dispensed them, Carr and Ann described the principal events of the past few days—the break-in and bugging at Purley's Cottage, Police Chief Timmins's self-serving theory that they had murdered Lloyd Cunningham, and Carr's visit that afternoon to the A. and S. Chemical Company and his subsequent smashup in the Volkswagen.

Arnold's frown grew deeper as the recital progressed. When it was over he said to Carr, ''At least you didn't get yourself killed today, that's something. You must have stirred Ritter up pretty bad—the question is why?''

"You told me a few days ago," Carr said, "that you'd try to get some more on his background. Have you learned anything else about him...or about A. and S.?"

"I've managed to pick up a few things," Arnold said, unwrapping the cellophane from one of his cigars. "Both Egon Ritter and his wife are naturalized citizens. Ritter was born and raised in West Germany, he's an industrial engineer, and seems to be a remarkably good one. For a while he worked in West Berlin. Then he found a better job and moved to Düsseldorf, where he met Maria Kopf, his future wife, who is also an engineer. They got married in Düsseldorf about seven or eight years ago, and shortly afterward came to this country to work for A. and S."

Joyce took a sip of her crème de menthe and said, "I shouldn't be at all surprised if this Egon Ritter had been in jail a few times back in Germany. Am I right, Arnold?"

Arnold shook his head. "No—he appears to have been a thoroughly honest young man. No criminal past in Germany. No arrest record. And he seems to have kept his nose just as clean over here."

"And how about A. and S.?" Carr said.

Arnold dropped a half inch of ash into a handy ashtray. "I didn't learn a whole lot that you don't know already," he said. "The company's medium-small in size, privately owned, manufactures a leading fungicide...and their executives seem to prefer a low profile. Maybe a bit unusual, but still perfectly kosher."

"Nothing else?" Carr said.

Arnold shook his head again. "No, not really. They've minded their p's and q's apparently. Never been in trouble. Our state tax boys haven't a word to say against them. Neither does the Commerce Department in Washington. Or any of the regulatory agencies I've talked to. The fact is, Alex, I don't entirely agree with your newspaper people in New York—the profit picture at A. and S. doesn't seem all that unusual to me—certainly not enough to make a federal case out of it. And otherwise, I don't really see what's suspicious about the company setup. In my judgment—though you might have a different opinion—they could very well be just another private operator, like hundreds of others, each one of them doing their best to suit themselves.''

It was Carr's turn to smile. He lifted his empty glass to indicate that he needed a refill, and he said, ''You're right, Arnold—my opinion of A. and S. is quite a bit different from yours. Maybe because I'm not just thinking about corporate balance sheets and the bottom line. I'm also thinking about a man in upstate New York who's lying in his coffin tonight. And another man here in Walton who almost got measured for *his* coffin today. Now one of the few things these two birds apparently had in common was their curiosity about A. and S.—maybe it was too much curiosity for their own good.''

''I'm not sure I follow you, darling,'' Ann said. ''Do you mean that today—when Ritter tried to kill you— he was acting to protect the interests of the company?''

Carr shook his head. ''No, I very much doubt that— Ritter was acting for himself—he was in complete panic. All I meant was that Lloyd's death, and my own near miss this afternoon, were both in some way connected with three things—with the A. and S. Chemical Company, with the product they make, and with Lloyd's discovery of the Amazon Factor.''

Arnold put down a fresh gin and tonic for Carr and

returned to his own chair. "Well, I don't think anyone would disagree with you about that, Alex— so how *do* you size up A. and S., and the fact that somebody decided to murder Cunningham?"

Carr took a swallow of gin and nodded to himself. He paused to light Joyce's cigarette, and then he said, "Sure, Arnold, I'd be happy to give you a rundown on some of my ideas. Let's start with Lloyd himself. We know that several months ago he stumbled across a curious phenomenon—an imbalance in the local birth-rate—that he called the Amazon Factor. He started to dig, and soon learned two things—that an accidental spill had occurred in Walton at the A. and S. Chemical plant, and the fungicide they made was responsible for the excess of infant girls that began to be born here, some ten or twelve months later.

"Next, Lloyd tried to learn as much about the company as he could—either to blackmail them, or to expose them in print. Because one way or the other he was determined to make a tidy little sum for himself out of his discovery. He consulted a newspaper in New York; he established some kind of uneasy partnership with Ritter; and he contacted the company president, no doubt to discuss money."

Carr paused and took another swallow of gin. "Now today, in his office, Egon Ritter told me that he hadn't been able to provide Cunningham with much useful information... and I tend to believe him. Nevertheless, by further digging, Lloyd *did* learn something more—something enormously important, and quite possibly criminal, about the company. Otherwise he wouldn't have lined me up to write an exposé of the story; and, of course, he wouldn't have been murdered a few days later."

"But did the company," Ann asked, "I mean, the people who own it, actually have Lloyd killed? As Timmins pointed out this morning, what kind of com-

party turns to murder just to cover up its unsavory or
illegal activities?''

"Any company," Arnold said, "that's either
owned outright by criminals, or else that has some
close Mafia connections. But if Cunningham talked
about the Mafia and A. and S. being hand-in-glove, I
don't think he really believed it. He didn't act
scared—and if he *had* been trying to blackmail or expose people like that, he would have been scared out
of his mind.''

"I agree with you," Carr said. "Lloyd did talk
about the Mafia—but I think it was just a smoke-
screen—he really believed the owners of A. and S.
were unscrupulous fat cats—rich but not particularly
dangerous entrepreneurs who'd bribed some official
types in Washington and committed a few other illegal acts. . . and he was going to expose them for fun
and profit.''

"But my dear Alex," Joyce said with a sigh, "if
criminals like the Mafia *aren't* involved in this
wretched company, then who in the world is?''

"Well, it's still only an educated guess," Carr said,
"but I suspect A. and S. might very well be owned by
a small group of men who are much richer and certainly no less ruthless than the Mafia. Think of them
as a national government. . . or better still. . . as the
inner circle of people who run such a government.''

"Sounds like it might make an interesting scenario," Arnold said. "Only you'd have to show me how
the pieces fit together before I'd want to buy it.''

"All right, let's run through what we already know
about A. and S.," Carr said. "The company was
formed a number of years ago. Discreetly. Covertly.
By men who shunned any and all publicity. Wealthy
men, too, because in time, they built three industrial
plants, along with the laboratories to sustain a successful research program. . . and we know that such

an industrial enterprise requires considerable capital.

"Now, none of that in itself was particularly unusual, but what followed *was* rather odd. Their profits remained low, but management apparently wasn't too concerned about profits. A foreign government, or people with large sums of money who were running such a government, wouldn't have cared much, either. Think of the ruling circle in a place like Saudi Arabia or Kuwait—or better still, Iran—a small group of multimillionaires, more and more eager with each passing year to transfer some of their wealth unobtrusively from their own shaky country to the comparative safety of the United States. The company, once established, would not only represent a desirable asset in itself, but would also provide them with an invaluable conduit to absorb more of their funds later on—so that it wouldn't matter much if profits were low for a while."

"All of which," Arnold conceded, "is consistent with the picture at A. and S."

"But then," Carr said, "seven or eight years ago, something else occurred—the company announced that it had developed an improved fungicide, and even though profit margins had previously been poor, a new and expensive plant was acquired in Walton. Now why did the company decide to expand just then? I think because the owners in question suddenly found themselves even richer than before. Infinitely richer. Remember that all of this took place seven or eight years ago—and then ask yourself what else happened around the same time?"

"My God, that's sharp, Alex, that's very, very sharp," Arnold said. "Of course, when you put it like that, the answer's easy. Seven or eight years ago— OPEC. When the oil sheiks really began hitting the jackpot."

"And don't lose sight of the way Lloyd was killed. The Mafia probably would have gunned him down publicly . . . but this was a very *discreet* murder. It took a bit of careful planning by old, experienced hands—like the men who once ran Savak, the shah's secret police. We may not know exactly who they are, but we can be certain of one thing. Lloyd's killers were no ordinary thugs, they were intelligent, highly skilled professionals."

Joyce sighed again and said, "Poor Lloyd, he didn't realize what he'd got into, did he?"

Carr swallowed the last of his gin and tonic and put down his glass. "No, he never had a clue, Joyce. He thought he was playing with a few rich, easily intimidated tabby cats, when in reality, he was tangling with a pack of man-eating Bengal tigers."

"And all because he wanted more money. I find that so difficult to understand. I mean, how hard up could Lloyd have been? He had a good job and a nice house. He belonged to the club, and he went to parties. Really, I don't see what he needed all that money for?"

"To get married again," Ann said quickly. She glanced at Joyce and Arnold, then shrugged to herself. "It hurt for a while, but now I don't mind talking about it. Lloyd was in love with someone he worked with at the hospital. One of the nurses there. They'd been having an affair for a year or two, and she wanted to start a family."

"I wonder if she's anyone I ran into," Carr said, "the day I went to his office?"

"Did you happen to meet Edith Warner?"

"Dear God, yes. The nurse in maternity. I thought she wasn't too bright."

"She was just out of her teens, though. Which is what Lloyd preferred."

There was a brief, uncomfortable silence. "All the

same," Ann finally said, "he didn't deserve to die."

She lighted a cigarette and looked at Arnold. "But he did die—he was murdered in cold blood. And except for Alex and me, nobody seems to care. As far as I can see, an innocent man is dead, and nothing much is being done about it."

"Something will be done...I promise you," Arnold said. "After we open Lloyd's box at the bank on Monday, and get the tapes he made. Once I know what he really learned, I'll be able to go down to Washington again. I know some people there—some of the right people. It might take a while...but sooner or later, whoever killed Lloyd Cunningham will be brought to book."

Before long they all stood up and began to make their way outside to the car. As Ann got in, Arnold said, "I'll be in my office tomorrow morning. Could you come by and sign some papers—Lloyd's estate— I've got an appointment at eleven, but by eleven-thirty I should be free."

"I'll be there at eleven-thirty," Ann said.

On the way back to the cottage they passed the scene of the accident, and Carr slowed down for a moment to look at the burned-out Volkswagen. By the time the cottage came in sight, he could hardly keep his eyes open. He locked up the place and five minutes later was undressed and stretched out in bed.

When Ann came in he was already half asleep. She kissed him and said, "I've picked me a smart man this time—how in the world did you figure everything out?"

"I didn't," he murmured.

"I mean about Savak, and the oil men."

"It's only a guess, love. Some of it may not be true."

"Then you don't really believe it all yourself?"

"Sure—for the moment I believe it all. Until something better comes along."

Ann put out the light. "I'm glad Arnold's going to try to get something done in Washington. I feel better knowing we're not completely on our own."

"Arnold's smart," Carr said. "But he can't work fast enough. There isn't time...."

She touched his bandaged cheek and kissed him again, but before she could say any more, he was fast asleep.

THE NEXT MORNING Carr got up at ten o'clock. Ann long since had finished breakfast and was sitting behind the cottage near the sycamore, working on his portrait. He brought out a cup of coffee and studied some of the sketches, and then went back inside to wash and shave.

Before leaving for her own appointment, she put a bandage on his cheek and stared unhappily at his bruised forehead. She wished him a pleasant—and useful—session with Jenny, and told him that after signing the papers in Arnold's office she would go over to the house on Willow Brook Lane to pick up her mail. "See you around two," she said. "I want to get back here early and do some more work while the light's still good."

Carr finished dressing and went into the kitchen to begin fixing things for lunch. He was thinking about Jenny and what he wanted to say when he heard the doorbell ring. He glanced at the kitchen clock. Jenny was early. It wasn't eleven-thirty yet.

And it wasn't Jenny at the door.

It was two men, each wearing a white stocking mask over his face. And each holding a gun.

They were inside the cottage before he knew what was happening. He was told to turn around and raise his hands, and he did—there seemed little point in arguing about it. Not with a gun pressing against the side of his head.

One of them said, "Do as you're told, and you won't be hurt. We're going to the kitchen now. Walk ahead of us. Slowly."

Carr's mind seemed to have gone blank. As he began to walk, he was aware of nothing except the violent hammering of his heart.

In the kitchen his hands were tied behind him, and then a chair was brought over and he was told to sit down. Suddenly he thought of Ann, and how lucky it was that she'd left when she had. At least she'd be all right—and then he remembered Jenny, and his stomach turned over.

He was wearing a pair of cutoff jeans and he saw one of the men stoop and touch his bare thigh. There was a small sharp stab of pain, followed by a stinging sensation. Then another stab, and he knew the needle had been withdrawn.

"What are you going to do with me?" he asked the man with the needle.

"Nothing to hurt you. You'll go to sleep for a while. Don't fight it—it won't do you any good."

Then he was told to lie face down on the floor. When he did, one of the men said, "Start counting backward. From ten."

"Ten, nine, eight, seven, six—"

"I told you not to fight it," the man said.

By now Carr was sure they meant to kill him. And to conceal their crime, they'd make it look like suicide. He felt immensely tired. One of the men must have turned on the stove. He could hear it hissing, somewhere far away. And then, the smell of gas. . . .

His head had begun to float—it was a rather pleasant sensation. The drug was taking effect. . . he thought of struggling. . . but what would be the

use . . . he couldn't do anything to save himself . . . he
no longer even cared. . . .

"Count again," the man said.

"Ten . . . nine . . . eight . . . ."

And just as Carr got to seven, the world went
black.

17

AT FIRST, everything was misty and confused. He was lying on his back . . . inside a narrow unfamiliar room . . . and when he tried to move, his arms and legs refused to stir . . . they seemed to be made of lead. . . .

A stout middle-aged woman hovered over him. Apparently she wished to turn his head, which made no sense at all. He closed his eyes, and considered the problem. After much thought he said, "Exactly who are you, madam? And what are you doing here?" But he fell asleep before there was an answer. . . .

Still later he opened his eyes again. The place looked much the same. Everything still seemed misty and confused. A piping female voice asked if he wanted his glasses, and when he said he did, they were placed in his hand. He put them on and turned his head. The female voice belonged to his niece.

He studied Jenny's anxious expression and then glanced around the hospital room. "How long have I been here?" he said.

"Since yesterday."

"It's Sunday then?"

"Yes. Early Sunday afternoon."

Her anxiety puzzled him. But then, so did a number of other things. He remembered the two men in their white stocking masks, and the gun against his head. And in the kitchen, the injection they'd given him, and his lying on the floor, with the gas hissing out of the stove.

"I know you were coming to lunch," he said. "Were you the one who found me?"

"Yes, Uncle Alex."

"And by then the men had gone?"

"What men?"

Her bewilderment was genuine. Oddly enough, though, it seemed to clear away a good deal of his own. "Look—tell me—when you came to the cottage yesterday, did you find me in the kitchen?"

She lowered her eyes to avoid his, and nodded silently.

"Lying on the floor with the gas on?"

She nodded again.

"With a hypodermic in my hand?"

"No—you'd left it on top of the stove."

"Jenny—I didn't leave a hypodermic needle anywhere. I did not—repeat, did *not*—try to kill myself."

She raised her eyes and looked at him. "Everyone thinks you did."

"Believe me, I'm not made that way. I'm just too mean and ornery to ever try suicide."

"That's what Ann—what Mrs. Cunningham said. Not the mean and ornery part, but she said it was something you couldn't possibly have done. And that's what I really thought myself, Uncle Alex—only everyone else said—I mean mom and dad, and the doctor and the police—well, you were lying on the floor, and there was the drug bottle and the needle, and you'd turned on the gas—"

"No—the two men in the kitchen turned on the gas."

"But what men? Who were they?"

"I'm not sure. All I know is they both had guns, so I had to do whatever they said. They gave me an injection to knock me out, and then turned on the stove and left me lying there, because they wanted people to think I'd killed myself. Only they didn't know about your coming to lunch...and saving my life."

"Usually mom's late for appointments," Jenny said. "I'm glad she brought me on time yesterday."

Carr thought for a while, and then he said, "Can you remember—when you got to the cottage—did you see anyone in a car or truck, waiting up the road?"

She shook her head. "I didn't notice. *Maybe* there was a panel truck, I just don't know."

"And after your mother left, you came inside?"

"Sure. The door was open. I rang and you didn't answer, so I walked in, smelled the gas, and looked in the kitchen. As soon as I saw you, I ran over and shoved the window up some more, and switched off the gas. Then I dragged you out the back door, so both of us could breathe fresh air, and then I called the Emergency Service and the police."

"You shoved the window up *some more*? The window already was open?"

Jenny's brown eyes grew wide. "Oh, wow—I see what you mean. Why try to kill yourself by turning on the gas, and then leave the window open?"

"Or try to kill someone else and leave it open? My two gunmen were shockingly careless, wouldn't you say?"

They studied the problem from every angle they could think of, but no satisfactory explanation suggested itself. Then he asked Jenny for more details, and she described the ambulance ride to the hospital and his overnight stay in the intensive-care unit. When the doctors had said he was out of danger she and her mother had left, but Ann had stayed at the hospital during the rest of the night. Jenny had relieved her in the morning so she could go home to the cottage to catch a few hours' sleep.

"I'm sure she'll be back here soon," Jenny said. "She told me she would. We just didn't want you to wake up in a strange hospital room and see some nurse you didn't know instead of one of us."

When Ann did appear a short time later, she sat on his bed and looked at him without saying a word. Then she began to upbraid him for the way he always got into trouble whenever she left him alone, saying he was more worry than a three-year-old. Finally she put her head on his shoulder and broke down completely.

Afterward, when she grew calmer, Carr asked where the nurses had put his clothes. For better or worse, he said, he was going to leave the hospital that afternoon and spend the night in his own bed.

The hospital staff had other ideas, though. The floor nurse said that patients could not sign themselves out whenever they pleased—and certainly *she* did not have the authority to let him go home. She left to summon the doctor in charge of the wing— who raised more objections. But Carr was firm. Already dressed in his cutoff jeans and loafers, he said he planned to leave the room in ten minutes' time, whether they had produced a release for him to sign or not. By one means or another a release was found and he executed it promptly, in an atmosphere of considerable ill will. A half hour later Ann had driven Jenny and him back to Purley's Cottage, the dismal specter of white uniforms and bare hospital rooms far behind them.

ANN DECIDED to take the Buick into Walton to buy some much needed groceries, so Carr and Jenny soon found themselves alone in the living room. "We missed out on our lunch yesterday," he said. "Maybe this would be a good time to talk about tennis."

"I already know what you're going to tell me," she said. "You agree with mom and dad, don't you?"

Carr looked at her, and then reached out and for a

moment took her hand. Her candor and directness touched him more deeply than he was prepared for. Perhaps it was the hammering he'd been taking lately, but, whatever the cause, her expression reminded him painfully of an innocent, half-forgotten world remote from his own.

"I'm sure I agree with them about one thing," he said. "I'd like to see you go back to school this year and finish up. I believe you should. Dropping out would be a mistake."

"I know that," Jenny said. "I've already decided to go back." Her eyes suddenly grew angry. "And you agree with them that my tennis is a silly idea— isn't that right? You think I should just forget about the whole thing."

"No," Carr said, "I don't think it's silly at all. But I'll tell you what I would like you to do—what I think you *must* do."

"Okay. Go ahead."

"You must attempt—and it's never easy—to be honest with yourself. Are you ever *really* going to be good enough to go out on the circuit and be anything more than an also-ran?"

"But how will I know unless I try?"

"At the camp this summer—were you the best?"

"At the end I was number two, Uncle Alex. And I'd improved more than anyone else."

Carr nodded. "It isn't much of a life if you're only number thirty or forty in the country. Scrambling around for a few of the leftovers. Missing out on college, boyfriends, parties. Dedicating yourself to something you're really very good at—but not quite good enough."

She didn't answer, and Carr said very quietly, "Don't try to make up your mind now—that's not what I'm saying. But think about it. Without deceiving yourself. Give it a hard look. And then, after school next year, see if you still want to try it."

She kissed him, gave him a hug, and when Ann came back a few minutes later and offered her a lift home, Jenny said okay, and they went off together.

Left to himself, Carr stretched out on the living-room couch, arranged a couple of pillows under his head and began to read the Sunday papers. The door-bell rang. As the unexpected sound echoed through the empty cottage before dying away, he experienced a moment of nausea and panic. Then the bell rang again more insistently. He forced himself to climb to his feet and walk past the kitchen to the front door.

Lieutenant McGill was standing outside. His thin nose looked red and chapped. He had a box of tissues in his right hand, and a bundle of blue cloth folded under his left arm. Carr invited him in and inquired about his health; then they helped themselves to a couple of beers from the refrigerator and carried them outside to the shade of the sycamore at the edge of the garden.

"I stopped by the hospital just now," the lieu-tenant said, "but they told me you'd signed yourself out and gone home."

Carr nodded and the lieutenant said, "I've read the official report on your accident the other day. Sounds like Ritter didn't like the brand of goods you were peddling."

"I'm afraid he didn't," Carr said.

"No chance to prove it, though. Everything in the Volkswagen burned up that wasn't metal. Including the line you believe he cut."

"I didn't think there'd be anything to go on," Carr said, "after I saw the fire."

The lieutenant's smile became faintly ironic. "And then yesterday, according to what I hear, you gave yourself a heavy dose of sodium amytal, turned on the gas, and attempted suicide."

"And left the kitchen window open."

"Really? I didn't read that anywhere."

"No. Jenny, my niece, just remembered it today."

McGill blew his nose and pocketed the tissue. "Mr. Carr . . . do you happen to be right- or left-handed?"

"Left. I'm a southpaw all the way."

"Interesting. I wonder, then, how you managed to give yourself an injection along the outside of your left thigh?"

"You mean it would be awkward?"

"Yes. I realize this sounds strange, but it happens to be the wrong leg for a lefty. So, either you used your right hand . . . or someone else did the job for you."

Carr took a swallow of beer and said, "Tell me, Lieutenant, what was the reason, according to Chief Timmins, that I decided to kill myself?"

"That's an easy one. You were suffering from overwhelming guilt and remorse because you and Mrs. Cunningham had murdered her husband."

"He's still on the same track?"

"Why not? He thinks it might lead to the governor's mansion." Lieutenant McGill sighed, touched his nose lightly and winced. Then he said, "A serious accident and a suicide frame-up—people still aren't treating you right, are they, Mr. Carr? Well, my boss isn't being too nice to me, either. Only this afternoon he gave me a fine new assignment—he asked me to run over to Mrs. Cunningham's house with a search warrant."

"And you found something interesting there?"

McGill's expression became tinged with contempt. "The chief thinks I did. In fact, it was exactly what he was hoping I'd find." He pointed to the bundle of blue cloth at his feet. "Care to have a look?"

Without waiting for an answer, the lieutenant stood up and unrolled the bundle. It was an ABC uniform. "I found this in Mrs. Cunningham's garage. Tucked conveniently away in a corrugated box under a pile of old clothes."

"Where anyone could have put it."

"Sure. Would you mind standing up and trying it on for size?"

Carr did, and was not surprised to find that the uniform fitted him perfectly. "Almost made-to-measure," he said.

"So I see." The lieutenant then produced a small white plastic box with Carr's name and address on the inner lid. The box contained a pair of contact lenses.

"This was in one of the pockets of the uniform," McGill said. "It would appear to confirm Mrs. Nichols's testimony—that when she saw the ABC man, he was not wearing regular eyeglasses like yours."

"I can tell," Carr said, "that you've had quite an eventful afternoon."

"So it would seem. Now just for the record, Mr. Carr... have you ever used contact lenses like these?"

"Yes, I bought a pair last year. They never were very comfortable, though, so after a couple of months I gave them up."

"Maybe you'd take a look and see if yours are where they're supposed to be?"

Carr went into the bedroom and searched through the bureau and the desk. When he came back, he said, "No, they seem to be gone. Obviously that box is mine, though. So I'm quite sure the lenses are, too."

"That's what the chief figures. When I called him this afternoon, he was very pleased. If only he could find Mr. Englehardt to put on the stand, I think he'd be ready to go to trial."

"No sign of Englehardt, though?"

"Not yet. Which is lucky for you and Mrs. Cunningham. Along with the fact that you've got a good lawyer working for you. I'd say Mr. Daniels knows a lot about local politics, which is why Ed Timmins would like to keep on the right side of him. All the same, the governor's mansion is the governor's mansion. So—now that the ABC uniform has turned up where it did, and with your box and lenses in its pocket, there isn't much except Timmins's fear of what might be on Cunningham's tapes, plus the missing Mr. Englehardt, that's keeping you and Mrs. Cunningham from a first-degree murder charge."

THE LIEUTENANT LEFT not long afterward, and when Ann returned Carr told her the latest news. For supper they decided to open the best bottle of wine they had, but it did little to relieve their despondency. The ABC uniform and the lenses seemed almost too much to bear—another piece in a puzzle they couldn't explain, another link in a chain of evidence that was going to put them on trial for Lloyd Cunningham's murder.

They went to bed early, but neither of them slept very well.

THEY ARRIVED AT THE FIRST NATIONAL BANK in Walton just before ten the next morning and walked down the stairs to the vault where they found Arnold Daniels and Chief Timmins already waiting. A man named Olsen, from the state tax bureau, was also there. At ten o'clock sharp, the vault attendant, Mr. Antobelli, swung open the imposing metal gate, and they all went inside. Arnold asked Ann for her key, and Lloyd Cunningham's safe-deposit box was unlocked and removed from its niche in the wall of the vault. Then Mr. Antobelli, carrying the box

before him like a chalice, led the way to a private
conference room. They all took seats around a table,
Mr. Antobelli departed, and Arnold slowly lifted
back the lid.

It was a small box, tightly packed with papers and
personal possessions. Under the watchful eye of
Chief Timmins, Arnold began to extract them, one by
one. He gave each item a brief examination, then
handed it over to Ann and Carr. They, in turn,
studied the item, and then handed it over to Mr.
Olsen, who jotted down a few descriptive words on a
yellow pad.

There was a gold watch with a hunter's case, a pair
of old-fashioned mother-of-pearl cuff links and an
onyx stickpin. There was a daguerreotype of a name-
less young bride and groom, made in a photog-
rapher's studio a hundred years before. There also
were two life insurance policies, a health insurance
policy, a homeowner's liability and theft policy, and
a copy of the deed to the house on Willow Brook
Lane. In addition, there was a rolled-up diploma,
issued by Princeton University, conferring a
Bachelor of Arts degree on Lloyd Alfred Cunningham; a long, narrow illustrated edition of *Tales from
the Arabian Nights*, inscribed: ''From Father and
Mother to Lloyd, on his tenth birthday''; and a 1952
menu from a captain's dinner on the *Ile de France*.

And that was all. The box was empty.

There were no tape cassettes. Lloyd Alfred Cunningham's safe-deposit box did not contain any.

18

THE PRESENCE OR ABSENCE of any tape cassettes was of no concern to Mr. Olsen, who finished writing his notes, put them into a leather case and then departed. Chief Timmins watched him leave, and tapped the stem of his empty pipe against his teeth.

"Well, that's a disappointment, isn't it?" he said. "I've been looking forward to hearing them—but now, it doesn't look like I'm going to get the chance."

"The tapes will turn up before long," Arnold said. "Lloyd told Alex he'd made them, so they're just lying around somewhere else, that's all."

Timmins said he surely hoped so, offered them all a dazzling smile, and then said a cheerful goodbye and left the vault. After Lloyd's box had been locked away again, Carr and Ann followed Arnold out to the street.

"I'll have another talk with Timmins this afternoon," Arnold told them. "He's plenty itchy, but I'll twist his arm. I can hold him off at least another day or two. After that—if the tapes haven't been found—I'm not sure anything's going to keep him from charging you both with Lloyd's murder."

Arnold shook his head, told them to call him at once if there was anything he could do to help, and then walked off in the direction of his office. Carr and Ann turned the other way and went into a luncheonette near the corner, where they sat in a booth and ordered coffee.

It took a minute or two for either of them to speak. Then it was Carr who said, "I'm afraid, during the last few days, I've formed a very unfavorable opinion of your late husband. He was a crook, and he was a liar—Christ, Ann, didn't the lousy son of a bitch *ever* tell the truth?"

"Only when it suited him," she said. "And he enjoyed playing games—like lying to you about where he'd hidden the tapes he'd made."

"If he actually made any," Carr said. "After all, let's be logical, darling—what proof do we have that he really did?"

Ann shook her head. "No, Alex—I know he made some tapes. I'm positive."

"But why are you so sure?"

"Because a week or two before the Slatterys' party he borrowed a tape recorder. I remember he took it into his study for a couple of hours one night. I was stretching some canvas, and I heard him inside, talking into the machine."

Carr stirred his coffee and then looked at his watch. "Okay, let's say you're right—where does it leave us? He might have hidden them in the house, the garage, his office—almost anywhere. It could take us a week to find them . . . and we haven't got a week."

"I know," Ann said. "All the same, what else can we do but look?"

They began by driving over to Walton Hospital. The receptionist remembered Carr from his previous visit, and of course she recognized Ann and knew she was the late administrator's widow, so they had no trouble gaining access to Cunningham's office. But an hour's search failed to turn up anything. There were no tape cassettes in the desk or the file cabinets, or in the closet where Cunningham had stored his office supplies.

After leaving the hospital they drove back to Willow Brook Lane and continued the search for the rest of the afternoon. They started in the bedroom, and then proceeded to the study; they emptied out clothes closets and bureau drawers; they examined the furniture—beds and tables, sofas and chairs—top and bottom, front and back—and came up with nothing.

By five o'clock Carr said it was time for a break. He made two gin and tonics, and they sat by the kitchen table, picking at a bowl of unsalted peanuts that stood between them. After a period of silence, Ann put her hand on his arm and said, "Love—I know what Lloyd did with the tapes."

He looked at her questioningly.

"He didn't hide them here in the house, or in the garage, or anywhere else like that. Believe me, I understand how his mind worked."

"Then where do you think they are?"

"He gave them to Edith Warner."

"His young lady friend at the hospital?"

"Yes—she's got them somewhere—though I very much doubt that she realizes it herself."

"The idea might have possibilities," Carr said. "What made you think of it?"

"Because I know Lloyd pulled the same stunt once before—on me. A few years ago, he got mixed up in a scheme to sell blood-filtering machines to hospitals, and there were a couple of papers he was afraid someone might steal. Of course—being Lloyd—he didn't trust the banks, so without bothering to tell me, he sewed the papers into the upholstery of one of our chairs. I only found out by accident—a while afterward."

"Well, God knows it's worth a try," Carr said. "Though even if you're right, finding out where they are—and then getting her to hand them over—could be a tricky proposition."

Carr called the hospital and was told that Nurse Warner was not there, she was next scheduled to go on duty at midnight. So he looked through the phone book, and tried her apartment number.

When Edith Warner answered the phone, she sounded as if she'd just woken up. She said yes, she remembered Carr and the article he was going to write about the hospital. No, she wouldn't mind seeing him, if she could be of any help. She hadn't made any plans for that evening, anyway, so if he wanted, he could come over now. And no, she wouldn't mind if he brought along a woman who was assisting him with his work—that would also be okay. When Carr mentioned Ann's name, she hesitated, but by then it was too late, she'd already agreed to see them and could think of no reasonable excuse to avoid meeting Lloyd Cunningham's widow.

It was less than a ten minute drive from Willow Brook Lane to the two-story brick building near Walton Hospital where Edith Warner lived. When she opened her apartment door, Carr was appalled at her changed appearance. The buoyant, cheerful young woman was gone, replaced by a dispirited childlike creature with untidy hair and red, puffy eyes. All too clearly she'd been head-over-heels in love with Cunningham, and his unexpected death had devastated her.

Ann sat on the sofa and told Edith that she knew how much Lloyd had meant to her—and how much Edith had meant to him. "Lloyd was very happy the last few months," Ann said, "much happier than he'd ever been with me. Believe me, I understand your loss—Alex and I are truly sorry for what happened."

Then Carr went through his explanation—he was still working on his article; Lloyd had made some tapes to help him, but the tapes hadn't turned up.

Had she any idea where they might be? Perhaps he'd mentioned them to her—perhaps he'd given them to her for safekeeping?

Edith Warner shook her head. No, he'd never talked to her about the tapes, or anything like that. "And if he had," she said, "I wouldn't want to give them back—I'd want to keep them for myself. Then I could still hear him talking to me sometimes. Lloyd had such a beautiful voice...just like an Englishman's...."

And then, to Carr's dismay, she began to cry.

Ann gave her a handkerchief, and Carr went to the kitchen and returned with a glass of water. She swallowed a little, and grew calmer. Then she began to speak of her feelings, and they made no effort to stop her.

"I miss him so much—I can't seem to think of anything else," she said. "Especially at night, when I'm alone back here, knowing I'll never see him again. I don't have a lot to remind me of him. We had some snapshots taken last year, so I get them out and look at them...."

Carr gazed around the room. One of the floor lamps caught his eye. The large base probably could be unscrewed—a clever place to hide a couple of tape cassettes.

"And last month, for my birthday," Edith was saying to Ann, "he gave me some beautiful matched luggage...."

Carr got up and walked over to the window. He adjusted the Venetian blind, then turned casually and studied the lamp. The base certainly was roomy enough. But it was only a hunch—half a dozen other objects in the room could just as well conceal the cassettes, and with Edith Warner there, how was he to examine any of them without giving the game away?

"...a vanity case, and a shoulder bag, too...."
she was saying to Ann. "Lloyd always liked to see me
use the bag, because he'd given it to me. And I still
take it with me everywhere I go, because it reminds
me of him and makes me feel that maybe he really
isn't gone. But now I'll never use the rest of the luggage, because we won't be going on our honeymoon.
We'll never get married and have a family, like we
planned to...."

The tears were ready to start again and Ann murmured some words of sympathy. Then she said, "Do
you know, Edith, I think it's very sad that you
haven't a few real keepsakes to remember Lloyd by.
You loved him—so his things would mean much more
to you than to anyone else."

Edith did not reply, and Ann said, "Look, I haven't
given anything of Lloyd's away yet. Why don't you
come out with Alex and me to the house now. We
can have supper and go through some of his things,
and you can keep whatever you'd like to have. If you
want to change before we go, Alex and I will wait for
you down in the car."

The two women stood up, and Carr dutifully followed Ann out to the street. They got into the Buick
and Carr said, "Darling, would you mind telling me
what the hell's going on? Back at the house you
thought Lloyd gave her the tapes, and now you pull
out of her place like a scalded cat before we have any
chance to find them."

"I guess you weren't listening," Ann said. "Lloyd
gave her a birthday present—"

"I know—matched luggage, a couple of bags, a
vanity case—"

"*And* a shoulder bag—didn't you see it, sitting on
the chair? She carries it everywhere. Lloyd knew she
would, he encouraged her to—so that wherever she
goes, the tapes go with her."

"But she doesn't know she has them?"

"That's right. I have a bag like that myself. The cassettes must be on the bottom, sewn in between the lining and the frame, where you'd never feel or notice them. So, love, when we get to the house, just give me ten minutes alone with it, and I'll have the tapes out and the lining sewn back, and she won't ever know anything's been done."

As they waited for Edith in front of the apartment house, Carr felt a twinge of uneasiness. A woman with jet black hair was walking by, carrying a shopping bag. After a few moments, Carr realized that he'd seen her somewhere before. He couldn't recall the occasion, though, and by then she already was at the end of the block, just turning the corner. Ann said no, she hadn't noticed the woman, and so, after trying unsuccessfully to puzzle it out, he shrugged and let the matter drop.

With Edith between them they drove back to Willow Brook Lane, and then, while Carr began to prepare a salad and some hamburgers, she and Ann put their bags down on one of the kitchen counters and went off together to the bedroom. By the time they all sat down to supper, Edith already looked more cheerful. She showed Carr the lighter and the cigarette case she'd accepted, and said that having them would mean the world to her.

After supper Ann stayed behind to clean up and do the dishes, and Carr went off with Edith to look through more of Lloyd's possessions. When a quarter of an hour had passed, he excused himself and returned to the kitchen. Ann was just putting away a needle and thread.

"There's only one cassette," she said. "I've got it in my bag."

"Trust Lloyd to lie—even about how many he'd made," Carr said. "But. . . we have it. That's all that matters. Once we've taken Edith back to town, we'll go the cottage and play it on my machine. You're something else, love. I found me a real smart lady, didn't I?''

It was after eleven when Edith put all of her treasures away in the shoulder bag and they drove her back to the hospital. She stood at the entrance and thanked them. Then she suddenly stooped, kissed Ann on the cheek, and ran inside, without looking back.

They'd driven halfway to the cottage when Carr thought of the woman with the shopping bag who'd walked past Edith Warner's apartment a few hours earlier. Only now, he told Ann, he believed he knew who she was.

"At the plant she had blond hair, though. Ritter's wife, Maria...."

"The black hair tonight could have been a wig," Ann said. "Do you think she was watching us?"

"Or watching Edith. On the street, I noticed her eyes. She has remarkable eyes, very green and penetrating. I'm sure it was Maria Ritter."

A few minutes later they reached Purley's Cottage, where Carr put the Buick away in the shed. Then they got out, unlocked the front door, and walked into the hall. Carr said, "I'll get out my machine and we'll listen to the cassette. After that we can make copies for Arnold and the police... and breathe a hell of a lot easier."

Then he switched on the main living-room lights.

Two things were wrong. A recorder—one much larger than his own—was already waiting on the coffee table.

And a man was sitting behind it, staring at them.

The resemblance was uncanny. Adele Nichols, Ann's neighbor on Willow Brook Lane, had been absolutely right. He was the very picture of kindly, benevolent probity—old white-haired Judge Hardy himself.

Carr took Ann's hand and held it. Then he said, "I believe you must be Mr. Englehardt?"

"Yes, that's right, Mr. Carr. Now won't you and Mrs. Cunningham please come in?"

And though it was posed politely as a question, Carr knew for certain that it was really a command.

19

"Before this evening is over," Mr. Englehardt said, "we must reach a decision on some extremely important matters. In order to do so, we will first have to listen to the tape cassette that you've just obtained so deftly from Miss Warner."

Mr. Englehardt paused to examine one of the creases of his elegant fawn-colored trousers. "And I'm afraid," he said, "we must have a few ground rules to govern our proceedings. For one thing, we will have to remain here inside the cottage until all of our problems have been settled. And there will be no heroics or theatrical gestures, please. As I'm sure you both realize, I represent a well-staffed organization—roughly a dozen of us are here tonight. The telephone is temporarily disconnected, the cottage is watched and secure. We are dealing this evening with what Lloyd Cunningham quite accurately termed the Amazon Factor—and believe me, it is no exaggeration to say that the issues involved could scarcely be more delicate or more grave."

Mr. Englehardt extended his hand, and at a nod from Carr, Ann reluctantly drew the tape cassette from her bag and gave it to him. It was strange, after that, to hear Lloyd Cunningham's voice coming through the speaker; life and death seemed to have become inextricable confused, and there were moments when Carr felt that an error had been made; that Cunningham himself was actually present in the room, enjoying himself enormously as he spoke.

For most of its length, the tape contained little that was new to Carr, and nothing that was startling. Cunningham spoke of Edith Warner's chance remark in the maternity wing of the hospital, and of his own subsequent efforts that had led to his discovery of the Amazon Factor and the involvement of the A. and S. Chemical Company. He mentioned a meeting or two with Egon Ritter, and he described the reluctance of the company's officers to disclose any material facts about themselves or their corporate activities.

They had already listened to one side of the tape, and were well advanced into the second when Cunningham's narrative took a fresh turn. "I was now certain of several significant facts," they heard him say. "I knew that the A. and S. Chemical Company was no ordinary commercial enterprise; that its shadowy owners were eager to conceal their own identities and the true nature of their business activities; and that their chief product was not only extremely hazardous to the normal development of human sperm, but that it had been widely ingested by American citizens for the past several years.

"At this point in my research," the voice went on, "a curious idea occurred to me. The company had been in operation for a long time. Was it not possible that during these years another accident had taken place at one of the company's older plants—an accident that had preceded the one in our Walton factory? If such were the case, the implications would be tremendous. And so, with this in mind, I aimed my efforts in a new direction.

"For once, good fortune smiled on the just, rather than the unjust. On a business trip south I found time to visit Calverton, a Baltimore suburb, and the site of another A. and S. plant, and while there, to search through the files of its local newspaper, the *Calverton Chronicle*.

"Almost immediately I hit pay dirt. A number of years ago a reporter for the *Chronicle* named Jefferson Dills had discovered a curious phenomenon: for some time past, far more girls than boys had been born in Calverton. Mr. Dills contended that an industrial spill a year or two earlier at the A. and S. Chemical plant had contaminated the town's water supply, and was responsible for the subsequent excess of infant girls. Mr. Dills further stated that the company's product, a leading fungicide, was hazardous to human health, and he had dispatched a communication to the Commerce Department to that effect. Finally, Mr. Dills promised that still more was to come—that in the paper's following issues the matter would be fully explored; there would be interviews with the company's executives; and the response of the Commerce Department would be disclosed to eager *Chronicle* readers.

"Well, I looked at the next several issues of the paper, but—mirabile dictu—the story had all but disappeared. There was no further mention of the spill or the offending company, no mention of the excess of infant girls. Only a single brief letter from the Commerce Department, stating that there was no cause for alarm. Mr. Dills had been misinformed; his statistics were inaccurate, exaggerated and totally misleading. And I noted something else that was equally curious. No more Jefferson Dills—his by-line had mysteriously vanished.

"So I dug a bit further. And I learned two additional facts. Fact number one: less than a month after the appearance of Dills's modest little story, the *Chronicle* itself had changed hands. It had been sold to a new owner. And, according to the county records, the purchaser was none other than the A. and S. Chemical Company.

"Fact number two: within a very short time after the appearance of his story, Jefferson Dills ceased to labor as a poor, ink-stained, but honest member of the press. Soon after his article had appeared in the *Chronicle*, Mr. Dills had changed occupations. He had become an employee—and presumably a well-paid one—of the A. and S. Chemical Company.

"I find that only one conclusion is possible, and it may be summarized briefly as follows: the company silenced its critics by buying them out; next, it secured the complicity of the Commerce Department—and doubtless of other departments of the federal government as well—by offering bribes and similar inducements. And then, no doubt through the further bribery of still other officials the company, although fully aware of the fact that its major product was a dangerous health hazard, proceeded to expand its sale even further by opening a new plant in Walton, the owners of A. and S. placing their own narrow, selfish private interests above the health and welfare of their fellow citizens and the country as a whole.

"What we have then, is a demonstrable, criminal conspiracy, cynically devised for personal gain, by unprincipled malefactors of great wealth hiding behind the A. and S. Chemical Company. Another Teapot Dome; another Watergate; a scandal that, once revealed, will rock this nation to its very foundations. And I, Lloyd Cunningham, intend to reveal it, and to bring these corporate sharks and pirates to the place where they belong. First to the bar of justice; and then to the cellblock of a federal prison. And this I will do, no matter what the cost, if it's the last single act I perform on this earth."

The tape fell silent, and after that, Lloyd Cunningham's voice was heard no more.

Mr. Englehardt removed the cassette, then looked toward the garden and gestured with his hand. The French windows opened promptly and two men entered the room. Mr. Englehardt handed the cassette to the shorter of the two. "Would you dispose of this, please?" he said. Then he turned to the taller man and said, "We'd like some coffee—I imagine you'll find the makings in the kitchen."

The shorter man went to the fireplace and crumpled a few pages of the Sunday papers. Then he broke apart the plastic cassette case, extracted the tape and, having unwound it, piled the resulting tangle on top of the papers. A match set the small pyre aflame, and within a minute or so nothing remained of the tape but a small pile of ashes.

After that the shorter man opened the French windows to create a draft and dispel the acrid smell, and by the time the air had cleared the taller man was setting a tray with coffee and three cups on the table in front of Mr. Englehardt. Finally he and his shorter companion returned to the garden, closing the French windows behind them.

Mr. Englehardt handed the cups around, and smiled benignly at Carr and Ann. "You have now heard Lloyd Cunningham's account," he said, "of both his own activities, and what he *believed* that he'd learned about the Amazon Factor and the A. and S. Chemical Company. The account is not without interest, but unfortunately it contains a number of Mr. Cunningham's personal misconceptions. It also omits a considerable measure of the truth—a good deal of which he was never even faintly aware of. Let me, therefore, go back to the beginning, and give you a complete—and truthful—account of the entire affair.

"I doubt very much if either of you," Mr. Englehardt said, "has heard of the organization that I represent—the Bureau of Operational Management, or BOOM as we sometimes call ourselves during our occasional lighthearted moments. The Bureau is part of the United States intelligence community, and was formed some twenty years ago. At the time it was felt that the Central Intelligence Agency, while an admirable organization, was growing a bit unwieldy. It was gaining an unwanted notoriety on the international scene, and certain of its departments seemed to be undertaking clandestine operations that were—to put the matter charitably—as pointless as they were inept. As a consequence, it was decided at the highest levels to form a small alternative intelligence agency—the Bureau—for the sole purpose of conducting a few extremely vital undertakings that it was believed the CIA and other established agencies were incapable of handling successfully.

"About twelve or thirteen years ago, the Bureau received an assignment to develop and test certain highly toxic chemicals similar to those that the Soviet Union already had developed, and that would be available for use against the United States and its allies in time of war. The employment of such weapons is always 'unthinkable,' so it is part of every large nation's intelligence and military policy to develop them covertly . . . just in case.

"For a cover the Bureau purchased a corporation that manufactured agricultural products—the A. and S. Chemical Company. The secret development of toxic chemicals could then be camouflaged behind the company's other publicly acknowledged activities—especially the manufacturing of a highly efficient fungicide, which A. and S. had just developed to protect America's wheat and other cereal grains.

"For two or three years, everything went smoothly," Englehardt continued, "until—as Lloyd Cunningham subsequently discovered—there was a small spill in the fungicide operation at the Calverton plant in Maryland. As a mere routine precaution, BOOM began to keep a sharp eye out to see whether or not the spill would have any negative local effects. No difficulties, though, were anticipated by the Bureau, for after all, the highly toxic chemicals had not been involved. Unhappily, the Bureau was mistaken. Eventually there was an unexpected development—a year afterward the birth-rate of males to females went entirely out of balance in an area adjacent to the Calverton plant.

"During the next several months—and, fortunately, well before the local newspaper got wind of the story—the Bureau conducted a complete, in-depth study of the unprecedented situation. We already knew empirically the short-term effect, when a massive dose of the fungicide was absorbed by sexually mature human males. Now we wished to answer several additional questions. First—and seemingly of primary importance—would the effect be permanent in such cases, or would human males return to normal reproductive patterns once the heavy dosage had been discontinued? Using a wide spectrum of ten different animal species, we ran a series of laboratory tests, and learned that, in all ten species, the effect of high dosages on mature males was only temporary, and that normal reproduction resumed soon after such dosages were discontinued. This result was extremely reassuring, for it suggested most strongly that our human males in Calverton would soon be able to sire infant boys at the normal rate again.

"But this was not all BOOM wished to determine. We realized that the effects of a prolonged, low-level ingestion of our fungicide also had to be considered, for such an ingestion had indeed occurred in America, on a wide scale, thanks to the general public's steady consumption of pizzas, white bread, and above all, breakfast cereals.

"The results of our second series of tests were a total surprise. For while the reproductive patterns of mature animals remained normal at every point, this was *not* the case for the immature animals. In nine of the ten species employed, *every single immature male*, on reaching maturity, could produce only females, and nothing *but* females. What this meant was inescapable... and appalling. Extrapolating the results of our tests, the Bureau reluctantly concluded there was at least a fifty-fifty chance that within ten years' time, an *entire* generation of young American males would begin to reach full sexual maturity—a generation that would be able to sire nothing but daughters."

Mr. Englehardt paused to let Carr and Ann take in his meaning. Then he said, "Critical decisions had to be made—and they were—in the highest councils of government. At first, a majority tilted in the direction of full disclosure. The consequences, though, promised to be utterly disastrous, both domestically, and in the realm of foreign policy, especially vis-à-vis the Russians and their Iron Curtain armies—imagine our country trying to lead the NATO Alliance with no American men aged twenty to forty!

"At this point, the Bureau offered a suggestion to the concerned officials. Why not suppress the story and, through the Bureau's operatives, place the Russians in the same boat as ourselves? The plan was accepted and put into immediate effect.

"The project was top secret. Needless to say, in order to protect the American public from further harm, production of the undesirable fungicide already had ceased at all three A. and S. plants, and a benign though similar fungicide was being produced and sold in its place. Now it was announced that a 'vastly improved' variety of the fungicide had been developed and would soon be in full-scale production at a specially designed plant to be acquired in Walton, and that before very long this improved fungicide would lead to tremendously higher crop yields throughout the United States.

"I need hardly tell you that this new wonder fungicide was a complete fiction—it was nothing but the old, undesirable fungicide that could not be sold to the public again. Instead, once production had been resumed, it would have to be destroyed—and as you'll soon understand—this destruction would have to be accomplished under conditions of absolute secrecy, after the fungicide had been shipped from the Walton plant, so that no one connected with the Walton operation—including the plant manager—would have the slightest idea what was really going on.

"Meanwhile, the Bureau—or A. and S. Chemical—had hired a leading East German Intelligence agent, Egon Ritter, to design and run the new Walton factory. He was given every opportunity to steal the production plans and formulas, which he obligingly did, transmitting them, with the aid of the Bureau, to East Germany and ultimately to his Intelligence chiefs in Moscow. Within less than a year the first Russian plant was in operation, and ever since then the original fungicide has been widely used throughout the Soviet Union, thus guaranteeing that after another few years of uninterrupted production, the Russians will have duplicated the American experience, and the international balance of power will remain unaltered. Granted, the effects in Russia will come a little later than here, but with foreknowledge we can devise contingency plans to cover that gap.

"During these early days, of course, Egon Ritter never realized what he really was manufacturing at

Walton, or that his entire production was being duly destroyed at another of BOOM's facilities after it left his hands."

"But then, unfortunately," Carr said, "there was a second chemical spill—this time here in Walton—and who should appear on the scene but Lloyd Cunningham, threatening to spoil all of BOOM's efforts."

"I'm afraid that's precisely what happened," Mr. Englehardt said. "First, Cunningham put Egon Ritter on guard, but we weren't too concerned about it. We knew that by then we had Ritter, and his Russian superiors, exactly where we wanted them. In fact, that had been an important element in our original plan. Just think what would happen to our Moscow friends if the affair ever came out in the press, or reached the Kremlin privately, and the presidium realized that certain members of the KGB, duped by American intelligence, had unwittingly introduced the Amazon Factor into their own country."

"So Lloyd appeared," Ann said, "and when he approached Egon Ritter, you decided to kill him."

Mr. Englehardt paused to refill their coffee cups, and to dispense the milk and sugar. Then he said with a sigh, "No, Mrs. Cunningham, you're quite mistaken. After considerable reflection, the Bureau decided to make a deal with your husband, and following extensive negotiations, we agreed to purchase his silence in exchange for the not ungenerous sum of one million dollars."

"But the deal came unstuck?" Carr said.

Mr. Englehardt sighed again. "Yes—not only was Lloyd Cunningham completely untrustworthy, he also was extremely grasping. He reneged on the arrangement and demanded still more money—a great deal more. And to see that he got it, he informed us that he'd engaged a skilled journalist who would expose the owners of A. and S. and their corrupt political friends. The price for his silence, and for yours, Mr. Carr, now being five million dollars."

"And it was then," Carr said, "that you finally decided you'd had enough of Cunningham?"

"There really was no alternative. All too often the demands of a blackmailer are insatiable—and our difficulties were further compounded by the distressing fact that Egon Ritter was having second thoughts about Cunningham's decision to raise his price. He had acquired a gun and was planning to kill Cunningham himself. The odds were high that he would do the job so crudely he would get himself arrested and alert the press to the Amazon Factor and to everything else that we at BOOM were endeavoring, at all costs, to conceal.

"So—however reluctantly—the Bureau did what had to be done. And there the matter rested, Mr. Carr, until you happened to notice the unusual condition of the Cunningham lawn, drew the correct inferences, and called the matter to the attention of the police."

"I *have* been a problem, haven't I?" Carr said. "Going to see Ritter the other afternoon and almost getting myself killed could hardly have fit in with the Bureau's plans."

Mr. Englehardt looked extremely pained. "Good heavens, of course it didn't fit in with our plans—we've never wished to see the least harm come either to you or to Mrs. Cunningham."

"That being the reason," Carr said, "why you instructed Mrs. Ritter, the same afternoon at the plant, to warn me to be on my guard against her husband."

"*Mrs.* Ritter?"

"Of course, Mr. Englehardt. I assume you didn't hire Egon Ritter back in Germany without first knowing for certain that his every move could be closely monitored once he had come over here. And what better way to do it than by having him marry a double agent, Maria Kopf—who surely must work not only for the KGB, but also for BOOM.''

"That's quite ingenious," Mr. Englehardt said. "And also quite correct."

"But it fails to explain why, the next day, you had me drugged and put in the hospital."

"Mr. Carr—believe me—the Bureau had nothing to do with that. Ritter was still in a panic the day after your meeting, and when he learned that you had survived the accident, and before we could get Maria Ritter to stop him, he and an associate came here to the cottage and tried to kill you."

Ann leaned forward and said, "Mr. Englehardt, the Ritters and their domestic arrangements are an engrossing subject—but why have you bothered telling all this to Alex and me? We already know a lot more than Lloyd ever did. So now, when the fine talk is over, what do you plan to do—arrange to have us murdered, too?"

Mr. Englehardt's eyes widened with astonishment. He put down his cup and said, "Good Lord, no, Mrs. Cunningham. How could you even suggest such a thing?"

Carr laughed and said, "Darling—you don't understand how the Bureau operates."

"That's absolutely true," Englehardt agreed. "The purpose of all this—of informing you and Mr. Carr about the entire situation—is to ask for your cooperation, and your promise of silence. The Bureau appeals to you both, as loyal Americans—we ask you now, as good citizens, to support your country's intelligence efforts, and to help keep intact the international balance of power.

"And let me point out one thing more," Mr. Englehardt said. "By keeping silent, you will be doing something else of great significance. Your cooperation will enable the United States to continue controlling certain high-level Russian agents—agents we can readily pressure into taking actions favorable to American interests—whenever our government deems such actions necessary or vital. Until the present time, the Bureau's plan has been a triumph—our finest hour—but it's a triumph that *must* remain undisclosed. You, Mr. Carr, are a seasoned journalist, so you know there always are certain stories that cannot be made public...and the story of the Amazon Factor is one of them."

"Well, *I* don't happen to be a seasoned journalist," Ann said. "Maybe that's why I think you're overlooking something important, Mr. Englehardt. A simple but ugly fact—you killed my husband. You and your Bureau of superpatriots calculatingly and without mercy snuffed out his life. So what happens if Alex and I see patriotism in a different light, and we decide we aren't going to condone murder... any murder? What happens if we refuse to keep silent?"

Mr. Englehardt shook his head sadly. "Mrs. Cunningham, that would be outright folly...and would cause both you and Mr. Carr considerable grief. If you keep silent, the criminal charges now pending against you will be shelved. But if you speak out, you will be charged at once with the murder of Lloyd Cunningham. And tried, convicted and sentenced to anything from fifty years to life imprisonment. The motive was your husband's insurance—the tape is gone, the ABC uniform has been found in your garage, with Mr. Carr's lenses carelessly left in it, and Mrs. Nichols will testify that I was at the house. And finally, I will swear on the witness stand that both of you did, indeed, hire me—that you told me it was only a practical joke—and that in all innocence, I then participated in your husband's murder."

"But the jury might not believe you," Ann said. "You could wind up with a long jail term yourself."

"Let me assure you, there is no chance of that," Mr. Englehardt replied. "At the very worst, I might be convicted as an accessory, turned over to federal jurisdiction on a technicality, and then released within a few days through the Bureau's influence. I might even have to take a brief overseas assignment—a slight inconvenience—but I won't spend the rest of my life in prison."

"So that when you get right down to it," Ann said, "we really don't have much of a choice, do we?"

Mr. Englehardt slowly shook his head. "The Bureau understands your feelings, Mrs. Cunningham. We sympathize with your doubts. Can the taking of even a single life ever by morally justified? We in the Bureau believe the answer is yes—that under extraordinary circumstances, when the well-being of untold millions, perhaps of mankind itself, is in the balance, then the destruction of an individual, or even of several, is unquestionably justified. And believing this, we ask you and Mr. Carr for only one thing—your silence. Nothing more. For the sake of your country, Mrs. Cunningham, and for the peace of the world."

Carr smiled and said, "I admire your persuasiveness, Mr. Englehardt—I suppose you're an example of today's Renaissance man—murders efficiently performed in the afternoon, eloquent speeches delivered in the evening. And yet, despite all your persuasiveness, one thing does strike me as odd—that arrangements of this sort so often seem to be made on the basis of the highest moral principles, while the victims themselves lie hidden away, in their remote and conveniently forgotten graves."

"Peace against war, Mr. Carr. Freedom—however imperfect it may be—against tyranny. And since that *is* the choice . . . may we count on your silence?"

Carr and Ann exchanged a searching look, and then he saw her nod curtly. "You have our promise," he said.

"The Bureau is grateful. And so is your country—infinitely grateful."

Mr. Englehardt turned and gestured to the garden again. Then he rose and carried the tray with the coffee cups into the kitchen. Returning to the living room, he packed up the recorder and said good-night. "I'll let myself out," he told them, and moments later they heard the sound of the front door being shut.

It was almost one in the morning now, but instead of going to bed they got out a bottle of brandy and set it between them on the coffee table. After a time Ann said, "I wonder how long I'll go on feeling like this? Angry, frustrated. . . and somehow personally violated?"

"For a while, I guess," Carr said. "It's a reasonable response. You've been pushed around, darling, coerced—why shouldn't you feel angry? But whatever the merits of the case, what chance did we have? They were stronger than us—we had to agree."

"I know. But I've been forced to condone Lloyd's murder, and it's not going to be an idea I'll enjoy living with."

"There's no reason why you should," Carr said.

"And Mr. Englehardt, who can kill so easily if the cause is 'just'—what other ideas go through his mind? Where does he live and what does he do when he's not working for the Bureau? What kind of man can he really be?"

"I hope—I like to believe—a good deal different from people like us."

Ann swallowed some brandy and said, "I wonder if you're right?"

Carr shrugged, and then after a time, he said, "I wonder about something else. I think Englehardt told us the truth about almost everything, but at one point I'm sure he told us a lie. He said I was drugged by Egon Ritter. I wasn't. It was the Bureau. That day in the kitchen one of the two men had a small birthmark on his hand. . .and so did Englehardt's helper tonight—the one who burned the tape."

"But why would he lie about it?" Ann said.

Carr drank some of the brandy and shrugged again. "I don't know, love. All I do know is that for every lie, there's usually a reason."

She thought for a moment, and then she said, "Do you mean, Alex, there's something important we still don't know?"

He nodded. "I'm almost sure there is. And for some reason that I can't begin to explain. . .I really wish I didn't think so."

20

THE HUMID AUGUST DAYS began to pass. Early one evening Joyce and Arnold stopped off at the cottage on their way to dinner. Joyce, especially, seemed in high spirits—perhaps because of Jenny's decision to return to school. And when Arnold finally had caught up on his work they were all going to fly north and spend a couple of weeks together in Maine.

Arnold admitted that he was tired; it had been a tough summer. "Too many lousy clients," he said, "looking for tax loopholes or a cheap divorce. But one thing anyway seems to be okay now—our chum Timmins has dropped the idea of bringing charges. The other day I didn't even have to twist his arm—he'd already heard from somebody in Washington. If I caught the drift, they've given him a real nice proposition— two years in congress, the nomination already set up along with some campaign financing, and if he keeps his nose clean while he's there, then he gets the pole position for the next gubernatorial sweepstakes."

They all agreed that Timmins would make a deplorable governor, and then Ann and Carr outlined their own plans—they were going to get married at the end of September and try living in New York again, sell the house on Willow Brook Lane, but continue to rent Purley's Cottage for weekends and vacations. A friend of Ann's was leaving to spend a year in Paris, and one day soon they were going up to New York to see how big her apartment was and it had enough light for Ann to work. If everything seemed all right, they'd sublet the apartment for a year and then have plenty of time to judge whether or not they wanted to make the city their permanent base.

Joyce and Arnold started to gather up their things, and Joyce said to Ann, "I hope the sublet is better than the other place you told us about, the one you had when you were going to art school."

"Well, I don't imagine she has any mice," Ann said. "And the plumbing *must* be better. Of course she has roaches; they own the city...."

After Joyce and Arnold had driven off, Carr and Ann returned to the back of the cottage to enjoy a last hour of evening light. The first fireflies were out, as well as a couple of mosquitoes, but Carr scarcely noticed them. His mind already had drifted away... Jenny back in school, and Timmins in Washington... Joyce and Ann talking about mice again....

Ann was shaking him gently by the shoulder—she was frowning....

"Darling," he said, "go inside and make us two drinks, and then come back and don't say a word. I need more time to straighten the rest of it out...you and Joyce just now...I remember at the club the other night, I almost had it...not the mice, for God's sake, and not the roaches...it was the plumbing that backed up...I know it was the plumbing...."

He took off his glasses and put them on the grass beside his chair, and then stretched his legs out and put his hands over his eyes. He didn't hear Ann come back from the kitchen, and the next thing he knew, when he looked around again, there were two drinks on the little outdoor table, and hers was half empty.

"Alex, are you all right?" she said.

"Yes—just give me another minute to unwind."

He sat up, rubbed his eyes, and put his glasses on. When he took a swallow of gin, his hand shook, and the ice cubes made a rattling sound.

"You seem so—I don't know what to call it. I've never seen you like this before."

"I've never been like this before," he said. "I must have—not blacked out, exactly, but I was somewhere else...putting everything together. Tell me—Lloyd died on Friday afternoon—do you remember the date?"

"It was the twenty-seventh."

"All right—I'll go to the bank tomorrow. I don't really have to—the whole thing's clear already—but I'll do it anyway, just to be sure."

He took another swallow of gin, and put down the glass. "You're an artist, love—you're sensitive to such things—tell me what I look like now."

"You look terribly sad," she said. "As if you wanted to cry."

"In Anglo-Saxon America, men never do. Not unless they've gone into shock. But you *are* perceptive—you read me clearly."

At supper that night he told her what conclusions he'd reached, and explained how the pieces of the puzzle fit together. She listened, thought about it for a long time, and then said yes, she knew he was right. And afterward, when they went to bed, she held him close and tried to console him.

"I've lost something. It isn't there anymore," he said. "I feel hollow inside."

"Tomorrow you'll know for sure," she told him. "And then, love, you'll need a little time—but after a while, once you do know, you'll be able to start putting it out of your mind." And when he said nothing in reply, she held him even closer, as if she were cradling a mute inconsolable child in her arms.

THE NEXT MORNING, after breakfast, Carr took the Buick out of the shed and drove into Walton. He entered the bank at ten, descended to the vault, and told the attendant, Mr. Antobelli, that he would appreciate a few minutes of his time.

Mr. Antobelli was most helpful. He understood that Mr. Carr was writing an article on the state's banking regulations and the records that every bank was obliged to maintain for the protection of its safe-deposit customers. Walton's First National retained such records for a year in the annex directly behind Mr. Antobelli's desk. Each time a box was opened, the customer or his deputy had to sign a bank form, stamped with the date and hour of use. If Mr. Carr wished to know, for example, whether or not Lloyd Cunningham's box had been opened on Friday, the twenty-seventh of July, Mr. Antobelli certainly could tell him.

"That should be easy," Mr. Antobelli said. He went into the annex and returned with a card file. After setting it on his desk and peering into it, he shook his head.

"No, Mr. Cunningham's box was not opened on the twenty-seventh of July, Mr. Carr."

"Then perhaps on Monday, the thirtieth?"

Mr. Antobelli looked again. "Ah, yes—that's different," he said. "You see, here's the form with Mr. Cunningham's name and the box number, the date and the hour signed—10:15 A.M., July thirtieth—and the signature of Mr. Cunningham's deputy, who took the box out."

They chatted a while longer about other safety measures employed by the bank, and then Carr thanked Mr. Antobelli, left the vault and slowly climbed the stairs to the street.

It was almost eleven o'clock when he entered a small commercial building on the shady side of McCarter Square. He was greeted on the second floor by a secretary-receptionist and told he was expected. But when he entered the large, comfortable office,

he saw that it was empty. He took a chair in front of
the desk and, while he waited for its owner to
return, he gazed about the room, and his eyes finally
settled on the expensive leather attaché case lying on
the desk with the initials A.D. stamped in gold near
the handle.

The door opened behind him and a familiar voice
said, "I'm sorry I'm late, but I got completely tied
up—hope you haven't been waiting too long?"

"No, I just got here," Carr said. "I came from the
bank, where I was checking one or two items with
Mr. Antobelli."

As the other man walked past him and sat behind
the desk, Carr pointed to the attaché case and said,
"That's an interesting piece of leather goods you've
got—especially the initials. I wonder who uses the
case more often—the elusive Archibald Dempsey—or
Arnold Daniels?"

"Who's Archibald Dempsey?"

"I thought you'd remember, Arnold. He's the chief
executive officer of A. and S. Chemical."

"I see."

"And therefore a highly placed member of BOOM—
the Bureau of Operational Management. I suppose he
might even be the man who runs the entire show."

Arnold Daniels tilted back in his chair and smiled
sardonically. "And when did you first decide I was
with the Bureau?"

"Only last night after you and Joyce had left. I suppose I might have realized it before, but until I was
forced to, I couldn't allow myself—not consciously,
at any rate—to think the unthinkable."

Arnold took out one of his thin cigars and began to
unwrap the cellophane. "By which I'm led to infer
that it comes as an unpleasant surprise."

"Arnold...I've known you for well over twenty
years," Carr said. "When I was fourteen and my

parents were dead, you and my older sister got married. I admired and respected you—and you made me part of your family. When your daughter was born I was her godfather. And during all those years—almost my entire life—you weren't the man I thought I knew. You weren't the man any of us knew.''

After crushing the cellophane into a ball, Arnold placed it in an ashtray and then lighted his cigar. ''And now, judging by your expression, you've come here to tell me that you don't entirely approve of my second career?''

''Some things aren't easy to approve of,'' Carr said. ''Duplicity. Violence. Murder.''

Arnold remained silent for a time. Then he frowned, and said with a quaver of anger in his voice, ''In my opinion there are two sides to the question. I've always believed so . . . and I always will. Okay, so I'll give you the other side, not because I think it's going to change your ideas, but just to please myself. I start with a simple premise. The world we live in isn't such a very nice place—it's filled with duplicity, violence and murder. Always has been, always will be.

''And somebody is always needed to do the dirty work. A lot of people don't like to admit that, so they fool themselves by giving things a fancy name. We don't have garbage men or undertakers anymore, we've got sanitary engineers and funeral directors. Well, whatever you call them, the sordid ugly jobs still have to be filled, because if they aren't filled, people like you, and Joyce, and my own children, and Ann Cunningham, the woman you're going to marry, and all the other fine people we see at the club, and at Saturday-night parties—all of our decent, fair-minded, idealistic friends aren't going to have a nice, comfortable, decent, fair-minded world to live in for very long. No, sir—not unless somebody collects the garbage and makes the funeral arrangements—sure, and works for the Bureau and gets his hands dirty when something like the Amazon Factor and Lloyd Cunningham comes down the pike.''

Carr nodded and said, ''I know the other side of it, Arnold. It's only that I wish you weren't the garbage man . . . or the undertaker.''

Arnold looked down and studied the top of his desk. ''Well, maybe after a while you'll get used to it,'' he said, the anger drained from his voice. ''I'm not only thinking of myself—Jenny idolizes you, Alex, and Joyce wouldn't know what to do with herself if you never came around.''

''I'll still come around,'' Carr said. ''In time we manage to get used to all kinds of things.''

Arnold got up from his desk and went to the cabinet by the window. He took out two glasses and filled them with ice, and then poured some Scotch into one, and some gin and tonic water into the other. ''I never drink before noon,'' he said, ''but today's an exception.'' And after they'd tasted their drinks he said, ''Tell me—as a matter of professional interest—what finally gave the show away?''

''I guess you might say that it was the plumbing.''

''The *what*?''

''Well, you see, Arnold, even after I'd figured out that Cunningham had been murdered, there was still something that puzzled me. I mean the way it was done—running the digoxin through the pipes and out the sprinkler—it reminded me of something else I was sure I'd heard a while before, only I couldn't figure out what.

''Then during our dinner at the club a few nights ago, while Ann was talking about her old apartment in New York and how the plumbing kept backing up, I almost made the connection. And finally, last night, she mentioned the plumbing again . . . and I remembered. It was you, Arnold, who'd told me about

Cunningham's scheme with the blood-counting machines, and how a hospital had to flush all of its sodium azide out of the pipes, or they'd be in trouble. Well, flushing out sodium azide and flushing out digoxin aren't all *that* different—so I asked myself, could you have planned Cunningham's murder and, without realizing it yourself, got the idea—subconsciously—from Cunningham's hospital scheme?''

''A nice supposition,'' Arnold said. ''And the way the human mind works it's probably true. All the same, it didn't take you very far.''

''Just far enough to start me looking in the right direction—in the one direction where I'd never looked before. And once that happened, a lot of things seemed to fall into place.''

''Like what?''

''Like the day Joyce came to the cottage and told me you had such a vital case on your hands that you'd postponed your vacation plans. Then last night I realized you'd never even mentioned the case, or complained about your latest unspeakable client, the way you always like to. That seemed out of character.''

''But if I'd been working for the Bureau on the Amazon Factor, then my odd behavior would have been accounted for?''

''Exactly—you couldn't leave town until the tape had been found, and until Ann and I had been neutralized. And, of course, you didn't have the sort of client you'd want to talk much about.''

Arnold nodded. ''Okay, the evidence is circumstantial but persuasive—so how did you build your case from there?''

''I took the big leap,'' Carr said. ''I assumed that it was you who'd planned everything from start to finish. And that you had three main problems—silencing Lloyd Cunningham without attracting attention, finding and destroying the material he'd put down on tape, and working out a way to deal with Ann and me.

"The first thing you did was to arrange for the digoxin, the ABC man and the rest of it. Then, after Cunningham had died—obstensibly of natural causes—you went after the tape recording. But Cunningham had died on Friday, the twenty-seventh about four o'clock—when the banks were already closed. As a result you didn't inform the bank on Monday morning that Cunningham was dead, and that his safe-deposit box ought to be sealed. Instead, you went to the vault yourself on Monday, at 10:15 A.M.—as I learned today from Mr. Antobelli. Being Cunningham's other deputy, along with Ann—a fact you'd very carefully concealed from both of us—you had no trouble gaining access to the box. When you opened it, though, you found that the tape wasn't there. At which point you decided you'd let Ann and me find it for you."

"Everything seems to be right so far. And then?"

"I really complicated things for you by discovering that Lloyd had been murdered . . . and by going to the police."

"Yes, you weren't a hell of a lot of help at times," Arnold said with a sigh.

"All the same, you dealt quite effectively with the added complications. I wish I could have been a fly on the wall, Arnold, when you had your first talk with Chief Timmins—it must have been one of your finest hours."

"You've worked that out, too?"

"No problem, really," Carr said. "I'm sure you planted the idea in Timmins's mind that Ann and I had murdered Lloyd. You told him about the insurance policies to get things started, and then, while pretending to do the opposite, you built up the case against us. And, not being too bright, he swallowed the bait whole, and walked out believing it was his own idea."

"Any half-assed lawyer could have done it, Alex. The man's a complete egomaniac. It was easy enough to convince him that he'd worked it all up himself. And the Bureau needed a quid pro quo. We had to be sure that after you and Ann had found the tape recording for us, there'd be an effective way to silence you."

"Without killing us?"

Arnold looked down and studied his desk again. Finally he said, "Yes—without killing you. Not everyone at the Bureau was too happy about it—but I cracked a few heads."

It was Carr's turn to pause. He looked at Arnold, and after a while he said, "For which we thank you. Well, to wind up my brief—you then strengthened the case against us by planting the ABC uniform and my contact lenses in Ann's garage. And since Mr. Englehardt would always be available to go on the witness stand if we proved troublesome, you had us in a complete bind, exactly as you'd planned. Then, over at your house, Ann mentioned Cunningham's girl friend, and you guessed that he'd probably given her the tape. That's when you put a tail on Edith Warner—I spotted Maria Ritter watching Edith's apartment. A couple of days later Ann made the same guess; we found the tape for you; Mr. Englehardt destroyed it, and we had no choice but to agree to terms—our permanent silence, in exchange for the murder charge being dropped against us."

"Yes, that's about it," Arnold said. "You've worked everything out very well, Alex."

"No—there was one thing more."

"Which was?"

"Englehardt lied when he said Egon Ritter had drugged me. That was the Bureau, too."

"Why do you think so?"

"Because I recognized one of them when he came back later with Englehardt."

"I see."

"And I think it was a rotten thing to do to me, Arnold. You had no need to strengthen the case against me, but you did. You risked my life anyway. I could damn well have died from an overdose of sodium amytal."

Arnold had finished his first cigar, and now he took out another and again unwrapped the cellophane. He lighted the cigar and said, "So that's why you figure I had you drugged?"

"I do. And I think it was unforgiveable."

Arnold drew on the cigar and blew out a cloud of smoke. Then he grinned and said, "Well, I'm glad to see you're not completely infallible, Alex. You left something out of your brief—I had you drugged for a different reason."

"I'd like to hear it," Carr said.

"Okay—you may have forgotten, but the afternoon before you were drugged, Ritter tried to kill you by sabotaging your car. He still had a gun, and I was afraid he might try again before we could get to him and cool him off. So, to keep Ritter from doing any mischief, I thought we'd better put you out of harm's way for a day or two, until Ritter could be brought into line. It was rough, and I didn't like to do it, but I had only a few hours to work something out. And the Bureau is one hundred percent reliable with things like sodium amytal. Believe me, Englehardt is tops—in his own line of work."

Carr thought for a while, and then he said, "All right, I'll admit it—I made a mistake, Arnold. I remember now, you left the window open—that's something I hadn't figured out—I owe you an apology."

Arnold Daniels shrugged. "We all make mistakes—no brief is ever perfect. I give you high marks for everything else, though." Then his expression changed, and he said with a frown, "You'll let us know about the wedding? I mean, where and when? Joyce says it could be at our place, if you'd like."

"I'll talk to Ann," Carr said. "I'll let her decide."

"Okay. But you'll remember—when you're back in New York—about dropping around once in a while?"

Carr looked at his brother-in-law, and caught a fleeting glimpse of the hidden man—the complicated stranger he was just beginning to understand. "I told you—I'll still drop around—you can count on it."

"Well, then," Arnold said very quietly, "that's all right," and he ducked his head to avoid showing Carr the true state of his feelings.

A FEW DAYS LATER an unmarked police car stopped at Purley's Cottage. Lieutenant McGill accepted a beer and sat with Carr in the shade of the sycamore, his back to the grinning leprechaun. He said he was finally over his summer cold, thanks to Helen's new regime of fruit juice, vitamin B-12, and Mexican honey.

"I brought these back for you," he said to Carr, and handed him a manila envelope. Inside were four electronic bugs—two taken from the cottage, and two from the now defunct Volkswagen.

"Case winding down?" Carr said.

"It seems to be. According to rumor, the chief has better things to do with his time."

"Like running for congress?"

"So I hear. And one day—if you believe rumors—maybe a four-year lease on the governor's mansion."

"You always thought he might wind up there."

"I know," McGill said. "You win some, you lose some. In your case, Mr. Carr, I'm happy to say I was wrong. When we found those first two bugs in the Volkswagen, I figured you might not be around too long.''

"I did have one or two close calls."

"But not lately?"

"No—not lately."

"It was always what I'd call an unusual case," McGill said. "And someday, after the dust settles, I'd like to hear your version."

"Maybe someday," Carr said.

"Helen tells me you and Ann plan to live in New York, but you're keeping the cottage here. So maybe we'll still see you around from time to time?"

"We'll be down for weekends and vacations mostly. And if you and Helen ever come up to the city, give us a ring. We can talk about crime . . . and maybe have a good fish dinner."

The lieutenant smiled and said, "Yes, I'd enjoy that. Fish in any form—I guess it's the smell that reminds me of the good old days with Lieutenant Rosenberg."

"He was a smart man," Carr said. "You do him credit."

"Well, I failed with the case, but I never thought I wouldn't. Once you get a whiff of fish—or politicians—you'd better forget it."

Then Lieutenant McGill finished his beer and began to amble back to the police car, and Mr. Purley seemed to watch him go, his smile as broad and derisive as it had ever been.

TOWARD THE END OF AUGUST Carr and Ann drove to New York with some of their things and left them in their new apartment. Then they walked west to the Stanhope, where they found Mark Watson, Carr's agent, already seated in the hotel dining room.

During lunch Mark entertained them with the

latest gossip from the literary world, and only after coffee had arrived did he allow himself to think of business. Then he looked at Carr and said, "Anything on the Walton book—how's it developing?"

"I'm afraid it isn't," Carr said. "I'd have been in touch before, but there wasn't anything to report except a negative. I'm afraid Cunningham led me up the garden path, Mark. Fiddled the figures—there never *was* anything wrong with the local birthrate—and therefore, there wasn't any book, or any multi-million dollar contract."

Mark shook his head and said to Ann, "You know, you're marrying a great guy . . . but a lousy liar."

"No—what Alex says is perfectly true. My late husband did fiddle the figures—it was his idea of a practical joke—the Amazon Factor never existed."

Mark smiled and said, "You're better at it—you do it quite well, Ann—but I'm too smart for that. Or too well informed. There *was* something in Walton, only Alex isn't going to write about it. Nobody is. I know . . . because a little bird told me."

"What kind of bird?" Carr said.

Mark signaled for the check. "A strange little fellow really. Name of Smith. Quiet, but a trifle sinister. He paid me a visit at the office a while ago. He said he was from Washington—sort of with the I.R.S.—but not directly connected. He asked about your book idea, and then he sort of suggested that I'd be much better off not handling it. Or talking about it. Not ever. Unless I wanted to have a complete business audit. The full, four-star treatment. And not just this year, either, but also next year, and the year after, ad infinitum. He left me with the strong impression that the Amazon Factor wasn't anything you'd want to write about . . . or that I wanted to try and sell."

Mark paid the bill and they all went outside, where

he signaled for a cab. While waiting he said, "Not to worry—maybe it's just as well. It's better to be happily married and not too famous than too famous and dead like Cunningham."

THEIR SUBLET APARTMENT faced south and east, and from the corner window, they could see the trees in the park below and the lights along the river. They stood by the window and looked at the dark autumn sky, and Carr said, "I like it here. Think you'll be able to work all right?"

"Yes, I'll have enough light," Ann said.

They were silent for a while, and then Carr asked what she was thinking.

"I was thinking about the book you aren't going to write," she said. "And about what could start to happen here, a few years from now."

"Maybe nothing's going to happen," Carr said.

"Is that what you really think?"

"No—I have a hunch maybe it will."

"A country with no young men in it?" she said.

"Two countries—and God bless all the lovely people in the Kremlin when they find out."

"If it should really start, when do you think we'll know?"

Carr looked at the lights along the river. "Well, another few years. Maybe—shades of Orwell—not too long after 1984."

And they said no more, but stood with their arms around each other, and thought about life as they'd always known it, and the curious sort of life that might lie ahead.

Be a detective.
See if you can solve...

Raven House
MINUTE
MYSTERY #5

On the following page is Raven House
MINUTE MYSTERY #5, "Artless Death."

Every month each Raven House book will feature a
MINUTE MYSTERY, a unique little puzzler designed to
let *you* do the sleuthing!

U.S. (except Arizona) residents may check the answer
by calling **1-800-528-1404** anytime from May 16 to
July 15, 1982. U.S. residents may also obtain the solution
by writing anytime during or after this period to:

> Raven House MINUTE MYSTERY
> 1440 South Priest Drive
> Tempe, AZ 85281

Canadian residents, please write to the following
address:

> Raven House MINUTE MYSTERY
> 649 Ontario Street
> Stratford, Ontario N5A 6W2

ARTLESS DEATH

Professor Fordney faced the house as he stood at the outer edge of the wide flower bed. Along its edge were two ladder impressions. Between them and the house lay the twisted body of Henri Buton.

As the professor raised his eyes to the window, he observed a woman in a green jacket furtively closing a wall safe.

After inspecting the tall ladder that had been removed to some bushes twenty feet distant, the criminologist entered the house, glanced into the living room and went to the roof.

"I was sketching up here—" white-sweatered artist Arvonne Buton indicated her easel "—while Henri—he is my uncle—and Alexis Randoff, my fiancé, pottered about painting the furniture, rearranging the flower boxes and building the arbor over there."

Fordney examined the half-completed arbor with interest as Arvonne continued, "Henri called that he needed more nails and laths and started down the ladder. Suddenly he lost his balance, let out a terrible cry and…and…fell."

"If he hadn't broken his neck on that rock in the border, he might not have been even seriously injured," Randoff added.

"How do you know his neck is broken?" the professor asked.

"Why…I…could tell when I…I…tried to help him."

"Did you otherwise disturb the body?"

"No."

"Did you touch his body?"

"No…no…I couldn't," Arvonne sobbed.

"The ladder—why did you take that down?"

"I knocked it over in getting to Henri, so I just put it out of the way," Randoff explained.

The professor observed a fresh scratch on Arvonne's face and said, "Buton's death was no accident. You are both under arrest."

How did Fordney know Buton's death was not accidental?

From **Minute Mysteries** by Austin Ripley
Copyright © 1949 by Opera Mundi, Paris

Raven House Mysteries

An exciting opportunity to read some of the finest in mystery fiction!

As a Raven House subscriber you will receive every month 4 action-filled, spine-chilling mystery novels, superbly written by talented authors who are all members of the prestigious MYSTERY WRITERS OF AMERICA.
You may cancel your subscription whenever you wish.
Should you decide to stop your order, just let us know and we'll cancel all further shipments.

COMPLETE AND MAIL THIS COUPON TODAY!